Praise for *Of Women and Salt*

An instant *New York Times* bestseller
A *Good Morning America* Book Club pick
Selected as an Indie Next Great Read for April
Selected for Roxane Gay's Audacious Book Club

"A true poet's novel: a painstaking attentiveness to rhythm and metaphor allows Garcia to sketch complicated, thorny parallels between mothers and daughters."

—*Los Angeles Review of Books*

"Garcia's work is a raw and unapologetic narrative of what it looks like when women are written into difficult situations, not for the sake of spectacular violence but to demonstrate how they can reclaim their lives."

—*Women's Review of Books*

"Garcia makes a powerful statement about how we draw on our roots to understand our place in the world, showing that no matter how much we may try to escape the past, it always influences the present." —*Real Simple*

"Garcia's debut is slim yet lush, imbued with a harsh beauty that reminds us that the cruelties inflicted upon women—and, in this case, Latinas—are historical constants."

—*Oprah Daily*

"*Of Women and Salt* is a novel built on individual rebellions against injustice that are both adamant and insightful, and in their crosscutting stories, the similarities are amplified. . . . In the end, Garcia resists any easy conclusions."

—*Ploughshares*

"[A] breathtaking narrative from an author whose voice is already as confident as [those] of more seasoned writers."
—*Pittsburgh Post-Gazette*

"At turns eloquent and exuberant, the opening voices of María Isabel and Jeanette sing, and the addition of the voices of Gloria, Ana, and Carmen creates a heady chorus. . . . The book dismantles a variety of myths, including the idea that Latinx people are a monolith and function as one unified body."
—*The Atlanta Journal-Constitution*

"Chapter by chapter, [*Of Women and Salt*] leaps through time and space, creating a taut, lyrical patchwork of characters, connected by blood or by circumstance, whose lives have been shaped by nature and [by] nations. . . . Garcia's constant narrative shifts, both daring and assured, are also purposeful."
—*Interview*

"[Immigration] is at the heart of Gabriela Garcia's debut, *Of Women and Salt*, but this sensitive novel also touches on a wider range of subjects affecting the lives of Latinx women, [which] transforms it into much more than an immigration story."
—*Bookreporter*

"With lyrical prose and haunting storytelling, Garcia explores the lives of five generations of Cuban women and a mother-daughter pair from El Salvador who are all impacted by immigration policies, political violence, and the intersection of class, race, and oppression."
—*Electric Literature*

"This sweeping story takes us from the Cuban cigar factories of the nineteenth century to present-day Miami as we see the ways betrayal, tragedy, and women's choices embed themselves in our histories."

—*Good Housekeeping* (Best Books of 2020 [So Far])

"Gabriela Garcia, a prolific poet and fiction writer, delivers her highly anticipated debut novel, centered on three generations of Cuban and Cuban American women."

—*BuzzFeed* (The Most Anticipated Books of 2021)

"This anticipated debut novel from Gabriela Garcia follows a woman desperate to discover truths about her family's history—even as its current state spirals out of control. Her search for answers takes her from Florida to Cuba, Mexico, and beyond, and reveals broad truths about things we know about ourselves and what we choose to believe."

—*Town & Country* (The 28 Must-Read Books of Winter 2021)

"Following three generations of Cuban women from Mexico to Miami, Gabriela Garcia's debut novel promises to be a sweeping tour de force about addiction, displacement, and the legacy of trauma."
—*Harper's Bazaar*
(24 Books You Need to Read in 2021)

"[A] gripping, accomplished debut. . . . An interlocking portrait of women striving, loving, losing, getting lost, and getting found."
—*Lit Hub* (The Most Anticipated Books of 2021)

"Beautiful and tragic, *Of Women and Salt* follows five generations of women in Cuba, Mexico, and Miami. A story about immigration, mothers and daughters, and the choices women make for their families."
—*Barnes & Noble Reads*
(Most Buzzed About Debuts of 2021 [So Far])

"A moving intergenerational epic tracing the lives of women in a Cuban family, Gabriela Garcia's *Of Women and Salt* offers an insightful look into the ways in which our family's past is constantly echoing in our present."

—Refinery29 (50 Books to Read in 2020)

"A testament to the enduring bonds of struggle and love that tie us together beyond generations and borders. Truly the work of a measured poet, as Garcia shows the power of form, language, and structure in creating enduring scenes and images that I will carry with me for a long time."

—Luis Correa, Avid Bookshop

"I love a sweeping, ambitious debut, and this novel about a woman's family, with examinations of contemporary immigration and trauma and motherhood, sounds just incredible."

—Emma Straub, author of *All Adults Here*

"The forces that shape these families are unmistakably patriarchal, capitalist, and colonial. Against these tides of injustice, mothers and daughters fight to stay afloat, clinging to the wisdom that 'we are more than we think we are.'"

—*The Washington Post*

"At the heart of *Of Women and Salt* are the sacrifices made by mothers so their daughters can have different lives— perhaps better ones. But daughters may make choices based on their own wishes and needs, and this possibility is ever poised to pierce a mother's heart. In this way, the novel is quietly heartbreaking."

—*BookPage* (starred review)

"Women's lives and voices are central to [this] sprawling, multigenerational saga of interconnected immigrant stories. . . .

Here are the grandmothers, mothers, and daughters whose intimate struggles to understand themselves and their connections to the past are brought to vivid life in Garcia's accomplished debut." —*San Francisco Chronicle*

"*Of Women and Salt* reads like poetry. . . . [It] spans generations and homelands and feels like a sprawling saga. . . . Garcia deftly dismantles so many myths about immigrant women and families." —*Vogue*

"Garcia is already an accomplished short fiction and poetry writer, but this novel shows she's also an outstanding novelist and an exciting new voice with a talent for bringing humanity to the page." —*The Boston Globe*

"Insightful without being didactic, and profound while remaining accessible, [*Of Women and Salt*] reminds us of the various forces that push immigrant women to seek self-determination." —*The A.V. Club*

"Deftly sailing from one perspective to another across the years, Garcia uses these women's voices (as well as a handful of others) to flesh out an enthralling and important story. It is a notable feat for a first-time novelist to broach such an array of significant themes in one work. . . . Garcia shines in her ability to ultimately emphasize the strength, the perseverance, of these Latinx women."

—The Nerd Daily

"Highly anticipated . . . [*Of Women and Salt*] traces a broad arc across time and distance, zigzagging from a cigar factory in nineteenth-century Cuba to early 2000s Miami and a detention center in Texas in 2014. The intergenerational narrative tackles immigration, addiction, and sexual trauma with ambition and a poetic voice." —*Elle*

"*Of Women and Salt* spans centuries and oceans, and as Garcia introduces us to the women in this family's lineage, she suggests there's always more to unravel. In other words, migrant narratives are more complex and entangled than we've allowed ourselves to imagine." —*Bitch*

"[A] beautifully crafted novel that explores the many variables and inequalities that make up the immigrant experience and the role that politics, privilege, and skin color play in the process." —*The Atlanta Journal-Constitution*
(4 Books to Read during Women's History Month)

"A powerful novel from an eye-catching new voice."
—*Bustle* (The Most Anticipated Books of March 2021)

"From the perspectives of several generations of Cuban women, this remarkable debut shines a brilliant light on the broken immigration system and legacy of trauma for the people who endure it."
—*Ms. Magazine* (Most Anticipated Reads)

"Wonderful." —*The Seattle Times*

OF
WOMEN

AND

SALT

GABRIELA GARCIA

FLATIRON
BOOKS
NEW YORK

OF WOMEN AND SALT. Copyright © 2021 by Gabriela Garcia. All rights reserved. Printed in the United States of America. For information, address Flatiron Books, 120 Broadway, New York, NY 10271.

www.flatironbooks.com

Designed by Gabriel Guma

The Library of Congress has cataloged the hardcover edition as follows:

Names: Garcia, Gabriela, 1984– author.
Title: Of women and salt / Gabriela Garcia.
Description: First U.S. edition. | New York : Flatiron Books, 2021.
Identifiers: LCCN 2020047459 | ISBN 9781250776686 (hardcover) |
    ISBN 9781250776693 (ebook)
Subjects: LCSH: Mothers and daughters—Fiction. | Cuban American
    women—Fiction. | Immigrants—Family relationships—Fiction. |
    Family secrets—Fiction.
Classification: LCC PS3607.A721833 O38 2021 | DDC 813/.6—dc23
LC record available at https://lccn.loc.gov/2020047459

ISBN 978-1-250-77670-9 (trade paperback)

Our books may be purchased in bulk for promotional, educational, or business use. Please contact your local bookseller or the Macmillan Corporate and Premium Sales Department at 1-800-221-7945, extension 5442, or by email at MacmillanSpecialMarkets@macmillan.com.

First Flatiron Books Paperback Edition: 2022

10 9 8 7 6 5 4 3 2 1

Para mi abuelita Iraida Rosa López

CONTENTS

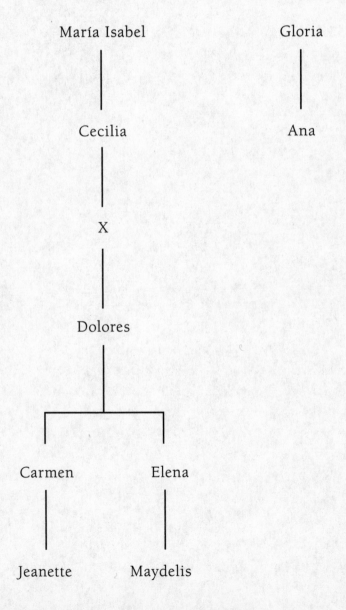

Carmen
Miami, 2018

Jeanette, tell me that you want to live.

Yesterday I looked at photos of you as a child. Salt soaked, sand breaded, gap toothed, and smiling at the edge of the ocean, my only daughter. A book in your hand because that's what you wanted to do at the beach. Not play, not swim, not smash-run into waves. You wanted to sit in the shade and read.

Teenage you, spread like a starfish on the trampoline. Do you notice our crooked smile, how we share a mouth? Teenage you, Florida you, Grad Nite at Epcot, two feet in two different places. This is possible at Epcot, that Disney tinyworld, to stand with a border between your legs.

Sun child, hair permanently whisked by wind, you were happy once. I see it, looking over these photos. Such smiles. How was I to know you held such a secret? All I knew was that you smiled for a time, and then you didn't.

Listen, I have secrets too. And if you'd stop killing yourself, if you'd get sober, maybe we could sit down. Maybe I could tell you. Maybe you'd understand why I made certain decisions, like fighting to keep our family together. Maybe there are forces neither of us examined. Maybe if I had a way of seeing all the past, all the paths, maybe I'd have some answer as to why: Why did our lives turn out this way?

You used to say, *You refuse to talk about anything. You refuse to show emotion.*

I blame myself because I know your whole life, you wanted more out of me. There is so much I kept from you, and there are so many ways I made myself hard on purpose. I thought I needed to be hard enough for both of us. You were always crumbling. You were always eroding. I thought, *I need to be* force.

I never said, *All my life, I've been afraid.* I stopped talking to my own mother. And I never told you the reason I came to this country, which is not the reason you think I came to this country. And I never said I thought if I didn't name an emotion or a truth, I could will it to disappear. *Will.*

Tell me you want to live, and I'll be anything you want me to be. But I can't will enough life for both of us.

Tell me you want to live.

I was afraid to look back because then I would have seen what was coming. The *before* and the *after* like salt whipping into water until I can't tell the difference, but I can taste it on your skin when I hold your fevered body every time you try to detox. Every story that knocked into ours. I was afraid to look back because then I would have seen what was coming.

1

DANCE NOT BEYOND THE
DISTANT MOUNTAIN

María Isabel
Camagüey, 1866

At six thirty, when all the cigar rollers sat at their desks before their piles of leaves and the foreman rang the bell, María Isabel bent her head, traced a sign of the cross over her shoulders, and took the first leaf in her hands. The lector did the same from his platform over the workers, except in his hands he held not browned leaves but a folded newspaper.

"Gentlemen of the workshop," he said, "we begin today with a letter of great import from the esteemed editors of *La Aurora*. These men of letters express a warm fondness for workers whose aspirations to such knowledge—science, literature, and moral principle—fuel Cuba's progress."

María Isabel ran her tongue along another leaf's gummy underside, the earthy bitterness as familiar a taste by now as if it were born of her. She placed the softened leaf on the layers that preceded it, the long veins in a pile beside. Rollers, allowed as many cigars as they liked, struck matches and took fat puffs with hands tented over flames. The air thickened. María Isabel had by then breathed so much tobacco dust she developed regular nosebleeds, but the foreman didn't permit workers to open the window slats more than a sliver—sunlight would dry the cigars. So she hid her cough. She was the only woman in the workshop. She didn't want to appear weak.

The factory wasn't large, by Cuban standards: only a hundred or so workers, enough to roll for one plantation a mile away. A wooden silo at the center held its sun-dried leaves, darkened, papery slivers the rollers would carry to their stations. Next to the silo, a ladder flanked the chair where Antonio, the lector, sat.

He cleared his throat as he raised the newspaper. "*La Aurora*, Friday, first of June, 1866," he began. "'The order and good morals observed by our cigar makers in the workshops, and the enthusiasm for learning—are these not obvious proof that we are advancing?'"

María Isabel picked through her stack of leaves, setting aside those of lesser quality for filler.

"'. . . Just go into a workshop that employs two hundred, and you will be astonished to observe the utmost order, you see that all are encouraged by a common goal: to fulfill their obligations . . .'"

Already a prickling warmth spread across María Isabel's shoulders. The ache would grow into a throb as the hours passed so that, by the end of the workday, she could barely lift her head. *To fulfill their obligations, to fulfill their obligations.* Her hands moved of their own accord. The bell would ring and she'd look at the pile of cigars, smooth as clay, surprised she'd rolled them all. She imagined the layers of brown melding into one another endlessly—desks becoming walls, leaves becoming eyes, and sprouting arms moving in succession until everything and everyone were part of the same physical poetry, the same song made of sweat. Lunchtime. She was tired.

———·———

A single dirt road in this town led past the factory's gate and continued on to the sugar plantation a mile down, both owned by a creole family, the Porteños. María Isabel walked this path home, one that snaked through the shadows and gave her brief reprieves from the punishing sun. She thought of Antonio's words: *Study has become a habit among them; today they leave behind the cockfight in order to read a newspaper or book; now they scorn the bullring; today it is the theater, the library, and the centers of good association where they are seen in constant attendance.*

True that since *La Aurora* had expounded the uncivilized nature of cock- and bullfighting, the number of participants had diminished. But it wasn't just the newspaper's recommendation that convinced them to give up blood sport. There were also preoccupations. Other workers talked about rebel groups rising up against Spanish loyalists. About men training in groups to join others headed west toward La Habana. María Isabel had been too hardened by her father's recent death, from a demonic yellow fever that consumed him within weeks, to notice at first, to care much. But then it was all anyone would talk about.

Though by the time rumors of guerrilla fighting had spread to their side of the island, so, too, had stories of infighting. Generals of the militias came and went, supplanted when their ideals became a liability. La Habana, with its manor after manor of Spanish families, looked toward the revolt with indifference, and it appeared more and more likely that the Queen would come down hard on any rebellion. For María Isabel, a scorching anxiety had long replaced those lofty early notions: *freedom, liberty.* She hated the unknowing. She hated that her own survival depended on a shadowy political future she could hardly envision.

Home. María Isabel's mother sat on the ground, back against the cool mud of the bohío. Aurelia had returned from work herself, from the fields.

"Mamá?" María Isabel alarmed to find her in such a way, an unusual blush spreading up Aurelia's face to the tips of her ears.

"Estoy bien," she said. "Just faint from the walk. You know I am less and less capable."

"That isn't true."

María Isabel helped Aurelia steady herself with one hand to the wall.

"Mamá." María Isabel touched Aurelia's forehead with the back of her hand, which gave off such a stench of tobacco juice that her mother winced. "Stay out in the breeze and rest in the hamaca, won't you? I'll prepare lunch."

Aurelia patted María Isabel's arm. "You are a good daughter," she said.

They walked to a hammock knotted between palms.

María Isabel's mother, worn down by decades of loss, hard work, nonetheless retained a certain elegance. Her skin was smooth, with hardly a line, her teeth neat rows unstained. After her husband's death, Aurelia had many callers, men with missing teeth and sun-weathered, papery skin who presented little in the way of wealth—a donkey, a small plot of mango and plantain trees—but offered care that she brushed off. "A woman does not abandon love of God, nor of country, nor of family," she'd said in those days, before the men stopped seeking her out. "I will die a widow, such is my fate in life."

But her mother grew weaker, María Isabel could see. Finding her daughter a husband had become an aggressive devotion. María Isabel protested: she was happiest in the workshop, in the fields, sweating over fire, peeling yucas and plantains and tossing them into a cast-iron cazuela of boiling water with her sleeves bunched to her elbows, catching pig's blood in a steel bucket to make shiny-black sausage, hacking open a water-pregnant coconut with a machete. True that cigar rolling was a coveted, respectable job—she'd apprenticed for nearly a year prior to working for a wage. Yet the factory paid her by the piece, half of what the men earned, and she was the only woman in the shop, knew the men resented her. They'd heard about this new invention, in La Habana—a mold that made it easy for almost anyone to roll a tight cigar—and feared María Isabel a harbinger of what would come: unskilled, loose women and grubby children taking their jobs for almost nothing. Suggested she might earn better keep "entertaining" the men herself. Took a greater share of her wages to pay the lector.

There were moments, like now, watching her mother lie red faced in the hammock through the window, when she pictured a world in which Aurelia wouldn't have to work, in which she spent her time caring for her mother instead of rolling tobacco with the men. And she knew with resignation that she'd say yes to any man who offered easier days. Such was her fate.

After lunch came the novels: Victor Hugo, Alexandre Dumas, even William Shakespeare; *The Count of Monte Cristo, Les Misérables, King Lear*. Some were so popular with the rollers their characters became the names of cigars: the thin, dark Montecristo and the fat, sweet Romeo y Julieta, bands adorned with images of jousts and ill-fated lovers.

They were at the start of the second volume of *Les Misérables,* chosen by a vote of rare consensus after the lector had finished *The Hunchback of Notre Dame*. The entire workshop had broken into applause at *Notre Dame*'s conclusion, for which Don Gerónimo, who ruled the workshop as though he were Notre Dame's wicked archdeacon himself, reprimanded them. But the workers cheered when Antonio disclosed that he had in his possession a Spanish translation of yet another Victor Hugo novel, this one spanning five volumes about rebellion and redemption, political uprisings, love, one that promised to move and enlighten before an aching conclusion.

This had been the least contentious vote in all of Porteños y Gómez's history. And now María Isabel spent the afternoons traveling far past the sugarcane fields and sea-salt-washed plantations to the hazy shores of France. In her mind, she walked the cobblestone streets of Paris, dipped her feet in the Seine, traversed the river's bridges and arches by carriage like a noble. She smoothed a gristly leaf between her lips, breath drawn in anticipation as police inspector Javert recaptured Valjean, the escaped convict. She thought of escape, of recapture. She thought of herself. Of what it would be like if someone wrote a book about her. Someone like her *wrote a book*.

"'A person is not idle because they are absorbed in thought. There is visible labor and there is invisible labor.'"

Antonio channeled Victor Hugo with fervor, as though their own labor, the rolling of tobacco, depended on his delivery. And in many ways, it did. María Isabel told herself that she, a young woman who ought to be home awaiting courtship, toiled in this sweltering factory because she'd been left an arid plot of land without a father or brother to provide. But she looked forward to each day, hungry for the worlds that opened as she hunched over her leaves, perfecting each roll and seal—news from the capital to which she'd been only once, announcements of scientific curiosities and denouncements of barbaric or dishonest plantation owners, travelogues from distant places she could barely imagine.

Also there were the gifts. She'd been on her way out and seen Antonio beside the foreman as Don Gerónimo read aloud the day's production and quotas. Antonio had tied his horse to a post and fixed a saddle on its back, something María Isabel had never seen but in La Habana, where the gentry did not ride bareback as in the countryside. That impressed her, and perhaps he'd mistaken her stare for something of another nature, because the next morning a strand of violet bougainvillea flowers lay on her rolling desk. And then, before Antonio began to read that day's news stories, he'd tipped his hat, looked her in the eyes, smiled.

She'd been afraid, of course—afraid that Don Gerónimo would see the flowers on her desk and call her out for indecency, perhaps garnish her wages or, worse, think her impious, increase his advances. Who knew what Don Gerónimo deemed permissible. His anger was of the untamable sort, unpredictable, without reason. He'd threatened her many times, once grabbing her by the back of the neck when she became distracted by a reading and slowed her rolls. He left finger-shaped bruises that lasted weeks. No man had defended her, not even Antonio. So she'd tucked the flowers down her collar. And in the evening, she'd shuffled out with her eyes to the floor, concerned that Antonio would look toward her once again and sure she would not know what to say.

But the gifts continued—a fragrant, ripe mango; an ink-pot with its delicate quill; a tiny filigreed brooch forged of metal. She would find them hidden beneath layers of tobacco leaves and conceal them as best she could. She told no one of the courtship and avoided Antonio's gaze, though at times he'd read an especially tender passage, and she would glance up for just a second, and always his eyes fixed on her.

And then she'd walked in one morning and there on her desk, unhidden: a book, its spine blue and rough to the touch, its pages a thin, smooth papyrus. She could not read the title, and she hid it beneath the ledge of finished cigars. María Isabel knew Don Gerónimo would think her presumptuous to bring a book to the workshop, accuse her of idleness, perhaps send her home, convinced a woman would never learn the strict norms required of labor. But she raced home for lunch, book tucked beneath her arm, and as she boiled yams over a wood fire, María Isabel fanned the smoke with its pages. When she was sure her mother wasn't looking, she traced the words, her fingers trailing the curves and abrupt edges of their shapes. It was like rolling tobacco, this need to follow the arcs and bends on the paper, to memorize the feeling. She hid the book beneath her bed.

When she met Antonio by his horse that afternoon, before he could say anything, María Isabel made her request: "If I could be so bold as to inquire, and forgive me the indiscretion, as to the title of the book you placed on—"

"What makes you think it was I?" Antonio's smile stretched his pockmarked cheeks. María Isabel instinctively gathered her skirt to leave.

But Antonio stopped her with a hand on her arm. "*Cecilia Valdés,*" he said. "A novella. I did not know you cannot read. I should not have been so presumptuous. I hope you'll forgive me and accept a sincere assurance I meant no harm by it."

"Why did you give it to me?"

"I will probably sound trite in saying you embody the protagonist, Cecilia Valdés. Perhaps that is why I am drawn to you."

She did not know how to respond, so she only looked away and said, "I must get home before dark," after which he'd asked her name.

"María Isabel, will you let me read to you?" he said.

"You mean to say outside the workshop?"

"It would be my greatest pleasure."

She handed the book to him.

"Thank you for an offer so generous," she said. "But I'm afraid I cannot accept."

María Isabel had thought she was ready to accept, to fulfill her obligation. *Can one learn to fall in love with a mind?* She regarded the bull-necked lector. How amusing that men thought they could so easily know a woman. She would wait until she couldn't.

———

Her mother was getting worse though. This she knew by a cough that doubled her over and shook her. Some evenings Aurelia so lacked an appetite that she retired early and left María Isabel to eat alone. And still her mother woke each day and prepared for her trek to the sugarcane fields. María Isabel pleaded with her, but Aurelia would work to the day of her death—and afterward if she could. This they both knew.

And then the war bled into Camagüey. Inevitable, she understood. Every year, *La Aurora* informed of more Cubans and fewer jobs; the economy increasingly concentrated on sugar, on plantations run on slave labor. Also in the paper: the abolition movement, Spanish taxation worse. She'd heard a wealthy plantation owner in Santiago freed his slaves and declared independence from Spain. She'd heard whispers of clandestine meetings. But she hadn't expected the fight to reach *her* life so quickly.

María Isabel woke one night to the sound of boots crushing

through vegetation and the light patterns of lanterns dancing on the walls. She peered out the window, careful to remain hidden as best she could, and made out dozens of men in the unmistakable blue-and-red of the Monarchy, their lapels bearing the colors of the flag. They carried muskets and swords, their faces drawn and weary, and she saw, faintly, what looked like dried blood on the breeches of some.

She couldn't sleep that night and clutched her body, heard the first far-off thud of a rifle, her mother waking across from her and coughing in fits all night. They spent two days like that, huddled in the shadow of their bed platforms, as though behind wooden shields. Cries and shots, metal hitting metal, men whose anguish echoed through the noise.

On the third day, Aurelia ran a fever, and María Isabel held her in her lap, wiping her face with a washcloth and whispering prayers to Nuestra Señora de la Caridad as her mother broke into cold sweats. On the fourth, the fighting stilled. Just as penetrating as the sound of sudden war had been, so, too, was the intensity of the quiet that followed, the stench of rot. They hadn't eaten in days, and so they rummaged through cans of sugared guava and fruta bomba and tomato they'd prepared months before, María Isabel spooning slivers into her mother's mouth as she lay supine. And when she was sure the silence persisted, María Isabel ventured out along the path she walked to work each day, now clogged with wisps of smoke, the smell of charred palm. She needed to find food. She needed to find her neighbors. In the distance, she could see fire, and she prayed silent gratitude it'd spared her home. She walked and walked through the quiet, listening for other people, for signs of life. Only the rustling of sugarcane and saw grass answered her calls.

Then, as she made a turn toward the riverbank where she did the wash each Sunday and bathed in the sun, she stumbled over what felt like a log anchored in the grass. She looked down and screamed.

A man, his open eyes to the sky and his mouth a permanent expression of disbelief, had his neck impaled by a sword, the pointed end emerging on the other side. Thick, coagulated blood pooled around his head and flies swarmed the wound. María Isabel looked up, past him, and saw it—a field of dozens of men just like him, left rotting in the heat, their innards and flesh unrecognizable, one giant mass of scorched meat, and as a final insult, a hog chomping through the remains, its face and teeth smeared in dark blood. She recognized the face of a fellow tobacco roller.

The grass quivered with María Isabel, oblivious to the carnage to which it bore witness. It began to rain and she stood there until a stream of red forced a jagged path to the river. Then she ran in her dress, torn and muddied and soaked, calling out to her mother as when she was a child, calling out to the giant unheeding span before her, and fell at the door of their home, her sobs heavy.

That night, her mother died.

———·———

Nothing was the same after the skirmish in Camagüey. Porteños y Gómez emptied to a third of its workers, the rest dead in the slaughter that had visited them or fleeing to la Florida, chasing rumors of tobacco factories offering refuge in exile. Don Gerónimo left, and Porteños, the owner of the tabaquería, began to oversee the work himself. The mood sobered, the readings changed.

On the first day back in the workshop, after the weeks of burials and rebuilding, Antonio took the lectern and announced that they would suspend the usual reading of *La Aurora,* as the rebellion had delayed its delivery to Camagüey.

They would finish *Les Misérables* after the lunch hour, and they would begin another novel, one by a Cuban writer, that morning.

María Isabel could not bring herself to look up at him. She concentrated instead on each roll of the leaves, on making tighter and tighter bundles.

"*Cecilia Valdés,*" Antonio began, "by Cirilo Villaverde."

Her hands shook. *Tighter rolls,* she told herself. *Tighter rolls.*

"'To the women of Cuba: Far from Cuba, and with no hope of ever seeing its sun, its flowers, or its palms again, to whom, save to you, dear countrywomen, the reflection of the most beautiful side of our homeland, could I more rightfully dedicate these sad pages?'"

Antonio's voice carried the workers through that dismal morning. It spoke of the Spanish and creole social elite; love between free and enslaved Black Cubans; a mulata woman, her place in their island's history. Even so, the author creole, an influential man. Not so unlike the other authors. After a lunch of hardened bread and bitter coffee, alone in her now empty home, María Isabel returned to hear a continuation of *Les Misérables.*

The days went by like this. Nightmares and crying fits gave way to tired collapse. And for whatever reason, possibly loneliness, possibly realizing she had no one left in the world, a month later she waited for Antonio and said, "I am not Cecilia Valdés." And then, "I would be honored if you would read to me from any text."

———·———

Once, as a child, María Isabel had accompanied her father to the city center of Camagüey to deliver baskets of a plantation owner's coffee yield to a market vendor. She watched wonderstruck as wealthy Spanish families paced the city's promenade, the women with their parasols and flouncing petticoats of fine linen, the children playing with hoops and sticks, and carrying schoolbook bundles. At the market, she watched enslaved women trail white women and gather their purchases, how the Spanish women would point and the Black women would gather, their dresses more like the country-side smocks she was used to.

She'd asked her father then, pointing to her skin, "Where are the people like me?" He'd hushed her with a smack. Children did not speak their minds, he reminded her. Children did not ask, children answered. Children did as they were told.

Now she knew the answer. The women were here, in these fields, some free and some not, some passing as creole. The not-so-whispered dictate of enslavers: mix to mejorar la raza. Spanish men, your violence is a favor, your violence is better-ing the race of this colony. So that someone like her could be told, you are not Black. You are mulata and mulata is mejor, and maybe your future generations will blanquear, closer and closer to white, take on the dictate as their own. Some plan-tations kept enslaved people, and peasants who earned their keep on small plots of land tended others. For their own rea-sons, the peasants and enslaved people, the guajiro farmers and criollo landowners, they all hated Queen Isabel II.

In the final days of war, the reports through the prov-inces grew more and more dire: public executions, entire villages burned to the ground, formerly free Black farmers forced into slavery. People were hungry, famished. Disease spread and wiped out whole families, whole prisons filled with mambises fighters. Their heroes were dying.

And still each day during lunch, for an hour, Antonio and María Isabel sat beneath the shade of banana leaves for read-ing lessons. Antonio read her poetry from Cuba's orators and political theory from European philosophers. Karl Marx, other men. They often debated. He taught her to spell her name, held a quill in her shaking hand as she formed loops and curves over a small scroll, and though she could not decipher the letters, she saw in the marks a kind of art, a kind of beauty.

"I have a special reading," he said one day. "Today, in the afternoon. A treat for the workshop."

"You'll not read from *Les Misérables*?" They were on the last volume, and its reading seemed the only event worth anticipating in those dark days when every sound of hooves brought fear of more loss.

"Yes, but first, a special reading."

María Isabel was still the only woman in the factory, now shrunken. The other rollers were fathers and husbands but also children whose hardened demeanor belied their innocence, who smoked puros larger than their hands. María Isabel knew to count her blessings—some of these boys had also lost entire families, had grown into men over one bloody night, had woken up the guardians of younger siblings, bellies rumbling.

"Today brings a rousing announcement," Antonio said from the lectern as the workers settled back to their desks. "One of our own great thinkers in exile in New York, Emilia Casanova de Villaverde—leader of the women's independence movement and wife of the famed author of *Cecilia Valdés*—wrote to Victor Hugo. Our beloved señora Casanova de Villaverde informed señor Hugo of *Les Misérables*' popularity in this, our tobacco workshops, that bring Cuba's artisanship to the masses. She informed him of the lot our women begin to occupy—how their hands, too, have taken up the work of men as they seek to liberate our island. I have in my very possession, a translation of Victor Hugo's remarks to his faithful admirer Emilia Casanova de Villaverde—and to you, the people of Cuba."

A murmur overtook the workshop, and Porteños lifted his head from his accounting desk on the second floor to note the disruption. But all were silent and attentive as Antonio unrolled a large scroll whose black ink filtered through the fibers in the light.

"'Women of Cuba, I hear your cries. Fugitives, martyrs, widows, orphans, you turn to an outlaw; those who have no home to call their own seek the support of one who has lost his country. Certainly we are overwhelmed; you no longer have your voice, and I have more than my own: your voice moaning, mine warning. These two breaths, sobbing for home, calling for home, are all that remain. Who are we, weakness? No, we are force.'"

María Isabel's hands shook, and she tried to still them, tried to still her rage.

"'Consciousness is the backbone of the soul. As the conscience is upright, the soul stands; I have in me that strength, and it is enough. And you do well to contact me. I will speak up for Cuba as I spoke up for Crete. No nation has the right to hammer its nail over the other, not Spain over Cuba nor England over Gibraltar.'"

Antonio trailed off, and María Isabel looked up to see Porteños stomping across the overlook and down the stairs, his face red and sweaty, the workers silent as he grabbed the papers from Antonio and commanded him to read from *Les Misérables* and only from *Les Misérables*.

Everyone had feared Porteños's arrival. Workers whispered that he'd broken the legs of an insouciant servant, that he knew about cigar factory strikes in the US and said he'd shoot anyone in his own workshop who dared complain.

"You are not to *incite* our workers with the imbecile ramblings of European artists with little understanding of the practical labor our good people perform!" he yelled.

Antonio looked at the crumbled scroll in Porteños's sunspotted hand. He muttered what sounded like an apology, turning so that María Isabel could see only his back. Her hands trembled so fiercely now that the tobacco fillings scattered across her lap.

Antonio turned, spun the pages of the book on the lectern, adjusted his glasses. He read from *Les Misérables* as though no disruption had taken place. He didn't look toward María Isabel once that day and rode off before she could meet him by his horse. And the words of Victor Hugo to Emilia Casanova de Villaverde reverberated through her that lonely night: *Who are we? Weakness. No, we are force.* She wished he'd read Emilia's own words.

———

Each week, there were fewer and fewer rollers in the workshop until only two dozen remained. Some had grown ill from diseases that spread after the fighting—obvious as they grew sallower each day, as they stopped smoking because of the labored breath that followed. When they stopped showing up, María Isabel assumed they had died or grown so sick they could no longer work. Others continued to save their earnings to secure their place on the private ships and dinghies that trekked to Tampa. The war made trade difficult too. Fewer cigars made their way out of the eastern provinces, though demand did not cease.

Antonio took on a different tone—seeking the most uplifting news from *La Aurora* to highlight, the paper finally reaching them, and suggesting novels that detailed adventurous quests, dramatic romance. When *Les Misérables* concluded, Antonio never mentioned Victor Hugo again. Voting stopped too. Now Porteños approved the readings, which Antonio spread across his desk each dawn, and María Isabel could sometimes hear whispered objections from Antonio quelled by a slammed fist on the table.

But at lunchtime, as they ate fruit and salted meat beneath their tree behind the workshop, Antonio shared his reserves. He read to her from Victor Hugo's second letter, printed in the paper—this one addressed to all the people of Cuba—in which he preached abolition and praised the Cuban rebellion against colonial rule, sending encouragement to the rebels whose numbers increasingly waned. Sometimes she cried at Hugo's words. More than once, Antonio gathered her as María Isabel shivered and shook in his warmth. She had found in Antonio a friendship she hadn't thought possible with a man, he of a gentler variety, seeming to relish in María Isabel the same spirit most sought to smother.

Behind the workshop, Antonio read to her from *La Aurora,* too. More and more each day, Porteños disallowed large portions of the lectors' newspaper in the factory. He was impartial to both sides of the war, but his were commercial calculations. Business was failing yet Porteños held on, sure that the Spanish would win, that resolution would come and, with it, a return to prosperity. So he held on, feigning loyalty to his gubernatorial overseers. And María Isabel began to realize why he censored *La Aurora*—the editors grew more alarmed at the repression overtaking the country each day. They denounced the tobacco factory owners who had banned the practice of lectorship as impeding the progress of culture, keeping workers calculatingly ignorant. Porteños determined to prove them right, she thought.

"They are careful not to write in favor of the rebels," Antonio said to her. "But the intimation is obvious."

The day Antonio asked her to marry him, a storm of fat, thick rain surprised them beneath the tree, and they ran for shelter under the roof ledge of the workshop. No one was around—not even Porteños, who went home to the plantation for his meal. Soaked, she unfastened the pins in her hair and let her curls loose around her face. He raised a hand to a sodden lock, and she pulled away, unable to look at him. She knew he was enamored of her; that much was obvious. But they had never spoken of marriage, and though he knew there was no one to ask for her hand, she knew little of his family, of his plans. Increasingly she grew wary of his intentions, wondered whether he saw in her a passing amusement and little more.

He bent before her, holding his hat, his own hair glistening with rain. "I know I have little fortune to offer," he said. "But I love you and promise I always will."

She said yes though she meant *perhaps;* wedding vows had long ceased to signal escape. She said yes because she had nothing left, and a learned man seemed as hopeful a prospect as she could conceive. And she sensed that he, too, sought a conciliation through marriage. In María Isabel, Antonio had found a way to flee without lusting after other shores, had found a reason to feign a braver face each day. She knew and, despite the weight of it, accepted her role as liberator of a frightened man. María Isabel thought it had always been women who wove the future out of the scraps, always the characters, never the authors. She knew a woman could learn to resent this post, but she would instead find a hundred books to read.

———

She moved in with Antonio's mother, a widow, and his unmarried sister. They were kind to María Isabel, but she knew they couldn't fathom why she continued to work. When she came home each afternoon to her mother-in-law rocking on the porch with a fan in her hand, María Isabel avoided her stare.

But how could she explain that the workshop had become deliverance? That mending her husband's chemise or pounding boiled plantains in a mortar without words, all the words from the workshop, would beat her mind to submission?

She cried for her mother, for her father, for her own lonely self as Antonio slept. She reached for him and wondered if the temporary relief of warm hands to grasp her own, trembling, was love. And she whispered the words often for comfort: *Weakness. No, we are force.* Now, they were her words.

———·———

The day the readings stopped was a sunny one, a bright one. Where she had struggled to see the leaves before her, that day a faint veil of light floated over each desk. The air was so thick, so humid, María Isabel barely needed to moisten her leaves.

She'd heard the mambises wore thin, that dreams of taking La Habana faded. She'd heard of families disappeared, of martyred fighters, of generals exiled throughout North America. Peace was coming, she could feel it, though peace meant surrender, slavery, so many dead for nothing.

Antonio was reading from the permitted sections of *La Aurora*. Its editors grew more abstruse each issue—they never mentioned *freedom* or *uprising* or *war*. But they spoke of self-determination. They spoke of culture as a means of liberation. They criticized slave owners and urged abolition. They told the workers to hold on.

And the workers did. Each day they took their stations and nodded at one another, transmitted courage in furtive looks. They walked past the empty workstations and blessed them. They gave up more of their pay to the lector, knowing there were fewer of them; offered fruits and bread to the skinniest among them; placed thicker cigars and fuller offerings of rum before the saints in their homes. Antonio's words comforted.

"'To Youth,' a poem by Saturnino Martínez, in today's *La Aurora*."

Oh! Dance not—Beyond the distant mountain
See how it appears
A fierce cloud which, blurring the horizon,
Announces a tempestuous storm is near.

The Spanish militia fighters did not make a large production of their arrival. A knock. Señor Porteños looking up from his perch. The workers met his eyes. He dashed down the stairs, wiped his face.

Three of them—slender, mustachioed men with handsome faces. They were there to deliver an official edict from the governor. The workers knew better than to stare, but María Isabel could see their rolling pause, could see how they all strained to hear.

Antonio folded *La Aurora* and placed it on the lectern as Porteños read the scroll before him and the soldiers watched. Porteños said the words under his breath and guided his fingers across the lines. Then, hand on the back of one of the soldiers, he guided them out the door, where they continued to huddle and speak in whispers.

"Gentlemen," Porteños said with a nod. The door's closing echoed through the workshop.

"There will be no more readings," he announced, matter-of-fact.

Antonio kept his eyes to the ground when Porteños led him out. María Isabel could hear them speak outside but could not make out the words. Antonio sounded agitated, and Porteños seemed to calm and admonish him simultaneously. Then, silence, just the brusque click of Porteños's heels as he reentered the workshop and walked back to his desk.

Everything in María Isabel told her to go after her husband. She closed her eyes and silently repeated the words that had carried her through past weeks: *We are force.*

She stood. She tucked her chair into the desk and walked out the door, knowing she'd never walk through its arched entryway again. A handful of workers followed. Porteños didn't even bother to look up.

———·———

They knew they risked their lives. But María Isabel and Antonio had ceased to care. Something greater than themselves swam in their blood; this would be their war.

Each day, when the workers who remained at the workshop had their lunch hour, María Isabel and Antonio met them in a clearing in the middle of a sugarcane field. Antonio struggled to receive copies of *La Aurora* now that Porteños y Gómez no longer employed him, but he rode into the city every few days to bring back other news. They made the trek to their meeting spot with a bundle of books each, philosophy texts and political manifestos, mostly. The workers repaid them with yeasty bread, with fat sausages, with cauldrons of ajiaco. On Christmas eve, they even slaughtered a pig that roasted for hours. Every day at noon, they lit their cigars and took a place on dried palm that lined the ground. They nodded and clapped at passages that inspired or put to words that which they all felt.

And María Isabel learned to read more each day. Now

that she had empty time at home, she sat with Antonio for hours, and when all had gone to bed, she ran her fingers over crisp pages by candlelight until the stub wore to darkness.

But still, they were dark days for her, filled with hunger, with panic, with mourning, even as she celebrated a secret: she was pregnant, her belly beginning to swell and round. She'd known for months before she shared the news with Antonio or his mother; she'd known even before she walked out of Porteños y Gómez. But she had kept quiet because marveling at what a life could be felt tenuous when death sank its tentacles into everything else. When she finally told Antonio, he lit up like wildfire in a field of grass, deepened his resolve to resist the terror the governor's edict had staked in their minds.

But Antonio didn't want her making the trip to the clearing with him any longer. He urged María Isabel to rest, take shade. Her mother-in-law agreed and made hot compresses of cheesecloth and cotton for her aching back, told her to mind her priorities. For a few days, she listened to them and stayed in the comfort of their homey cabin, stewing beans and embroidering a baby bonnet. But even in her state, she yearned to leave. She made the trips until her ankles could no longer tolerate them. And then she put aside all her housework and read for hours.

She could now string letters into words. She marveled at the magic of it all, how human beings had thought to etch markings on stone to tell their stories, sensed each lifetime too grand, too interesting, not to document. She placed one hand to her belly and felt the *something* in her move and stretch as if seeking its own freedom, felt as if the whole world were her womb. She wanted to write her own words. She wanted to write her life into existence and endure. Perhaps a piece of her knew death crouched close.

How did the soldiers find out? No one would ever know for certain, though they would speculate: perhaps Antonio had left behind compromising evidence at Porteños y Gómez (the translated letter from Victor Hugo?) and Porteños denounced him, perhaps a worker had betrayed him, perhaps it was simple bad luck—the soldiers marching through the field and finding the clearing, hearing the voices, the words.

The four soldiers were kind enough to let the workers go after they disrupted the lesson with whip cracks, a pistol shot. But they stood Antonio atop one of his fat books. One said, "Now will your literature save you?" Antonio clasped his hands behind his back, looked up.

And María Isabel, as though she knew, collapsed on the floor of their home, moaning, watching the liquid burst beneath her. She gripped her sister-in-law's hand and screamed, beseeched the santos. She let Antonio's mother wipe her brow and pray before her. She called the names of everyone she'd loved and lost.

"Declare your loyalty to the Crown," the soldier in the field said, rifle pointed at Antonio's head.

"Libertad!" Antonio yelled, loud enough that he hoped María Isabel would hear, that she would know he'd fight until the end.

But the world was going silent for María Isabel as she strained with the little strength left in her. She tasted the salt of her sweat and pushed and grasped at all before her, saw the room undulate, felt the waves crash inside. She heard her mother-in-law and sister-in-law's voices as if sieved through layers and felt herself go in and out of consciousness. Her fingers brushed against the stickiness of her own blood.

María Isabel felt her mother-in-law grasp at the fleshy head that emerged. And she heard her own pulse inside her, loud, multiplying as if fighting for two, for three, rippling. *We are force.* The resounding scream of life rushing out of her.

A soldier commanded his fellow men to raise their rifles. Antonio cried out again.

There was a click. There was a "Fire!"

The baby's wailing mixed with the firecracker sounds of guns ablaze, yelling to the sky. Antonio's mother cut the cord, placed the wriggling infant in María Isabel's arms, wrapped a blanket over mother and child. But María Isabel pulled herself to stand on wobbly legs. Weak, smeared with blood and sweat, trembling. The baby cried out again, and she held it close to her heart, tried to remember the feeling of her mother's arms as a child. Cecilia. She rocked her to exhaustion, watched as her tiny lids fluttered into sleep, never taking her eyes off the field framed in the window. Antonio's sister had gone to look for him. But María Isabel already knew the task would prove fruitless. She had felt the truth of the moment in her bones, in her breath. And she thought she had heard it: a faint, barely audible cry for liberty.

She brought Cecilia to her chest as tears clouded her vision, and the infant's newly found screams quieted when she felt the nipple and suckled. María Isabel had worried her milk sparse since regular meals had become an increasingly rare luxury. She fought anxiety over what solid food she could provide when the moment came. Instead, María Isabel fixed on a ribbon of smoke outside as it curled into itself, formed a slow waltz upward. She could think only of a cigar ashing on the edge of a life, could almost feel the warmth of its dark, woody embrace. But just like that, the sky was clear again.

2

EVERYTHING IS HOLDING YOU NOW

Jeanette
Miami, 2014

Blue and red lights disco-dancing across the walls wake her; she watches from her bedroom window. A white van with an official-looking crest. Two agents in black jackets with reflective letters. She shrinks behind the curtain. Only a sliver of scene is visible, and the only light on the street that hasn't burned out blazes a cold glow. The letters on the jackets seem to spell out the feeling of the night: ICE. Jeanette clutches her bathrobe tight.

The neighbor woman is walked out in handcuffs, wearing pajamas. On her pants, Minnie Mouse stands on tiptoe with fingers clasped at her face, hearts of varying sizes exploding in the air around her mouse ears. Jeanette doesn't know her. Just knows that she works every day, even Sundays. She sees her leave her house always in the same pink smock, with the same caddy of cleaning supplies. Jeanette's breath creates little spirals of fog on the window. One agent, a woman with a burst of auburn curls, shrugs her jacket closed with one hand while the other holds the chain that links the woman's handcuffs. No shouts, no screams, no tussle. The agents and the neighbor woman walk in silence to the van, lights still spinning like Fourth of July fireworks. The male agent slides the door shut with a bang. The rumble of the engine. The cloud puff of exhaust. Tiny wires crisscross all the windows, so Jeanette cannot see inside the van, cannot see the neighbor woman as the van drives down the road past every blacked-out town house window and makes a right, disappears. It all happens in minutes.

Jeanette tries to fall back asleep but cannot. She rubs lavender oil on her wrists, takes a tab of melatonin. Lies there, eyes open, for what feels like an hour. Finally she dials the number, making sure to press *67 first to disable caller ID. Mario answers in a sleep-clogged voice. Mario answers because Mario always answers no matter the time of night. And even now, six months separated and six months sober, Jeanette still swallows the rock in her throat as she waits for the click, the familiar voice.

She says: "I miss you."

No need for pleasantries or pretense. No need to even announce herself. Of course it is her. A sigh on the other side. A rustling of sheets.

"Jeanette."

"Hi."

"We can't keep doing this."

"I can't sleep."

A sound like a snap. Turning on a light?

"That brand of ginger ale that you like," she says. "The one they stopped selling at the supermarket near our old house? I saw it today where I shop."

"Where do you shop?"

"You know I can't tell you that."

"At least tell me you're still in Miami?"

Silence.

A sigh.

"Jeanette, how long are we going to play games like this? If you won't even tell me where you are, do you call just to break my heart even more? Just to make it harder for me?"

She can picture him. He sleeps shirtless and in boxers. She can picture the print of the sheets, the color, the smell of just-washed. The pile of library books on his nightstand. The color of the walls. They picked it out together: Eggshell Bavarian Cream. What's he reading these days?

He says: "Just tell me you are okay."

She says: "I am okay."

She thought she was calling him to talk about the raid, the neighbor woman. Turns out she has nothing to say about that. Also turns out: sobriety is a daily exercise, especially at night. She pictures her nightstand of just a year ago: crushed OxyContins, grapey cough syrup to send her pain-free into morning. A kind of prayer. She pulls the covers to her chin. Wonders what real prayer she'd whisper if she were the kind of woman who prayed.

———·———

What she knows about the neighbor woman: likely in her thirties, probably Central American, comes home each evening around six or seven. She has burnt-sugar skin and dark black hair. Always her face is perfectly made up. Arched eyebrows. Deep brown lips. Eyelashes that curl up like flower petals. Unmarried? Jeanette has never seen her with anyone, not even a friend. Just a young daughter who gets dropped off every night around eight. What happened to the daughter? She realizes she hasn't thought about the daughter. The driver who drops off the daughter never gets out of the car. Every day the little girl just runs up to her door and knocks. She is around seven or eight years old, Jeanette guesses.

Occasionally their paths cross when she and the neighbor woman are at their driveways. They say hello to each other, the daughter smiles. They've never talked more than that. Jeanette is twenty-seven, and she hardly notices or thinks about children.

And now, after the raid, the blood orange of a Miami morning like any other. Of course she is still in Miami. These streets course through the blood—all pastel mini-mall suburban blight, tropical flourish to each dragging second, each concrete bungalow a kind of American dream achieved no matter how crooked the mortgage. No other place calls her home like this. It's just another day in another home not that different from the one she shared with Mario, only Mario isn't here.

Jeanette sets her laptop on the kitchen table beside the window. This gives her a view of the neighbor's house. All day she sits with her headphones on, listening to a psychiatrist define patients by insurance number and ailment. Obsessive-compulsive disorder. Hypomania. Schizotypal personality co-occurring with generalized social phobia. She types furiously, occasionally pausing the tape to search her *DSM* for spelling and billing codes. She makes a note to order the newest version. She microwaves a Healthy and Lean meatball parmesan with a side of matchstick veggies. She smokes cigarette after cigarette even though her sponsor has warned her to stop because "reliance on *any* substance or drug is a slippery slope to relapse." As if everyone in recovery doesn't smoke. Outside: silence falls, a slow domino effect, cars leaving their driveways until the street is empty of all but Jeanette's. A few rustling trees. An occasional lizard or bird. No sign of the neighbor woman. No sign that anything at all happened the night before.

By evening Jeanette has finished her transcription work,

has emailed it to her temp agency. She readies for dinner, browses the freezer, hums a top 40 tune, Rihanna or Beyoncé or Adele. She glimpses a car driving up to the neighbor's house. The neighbor's daughter gets out, and the car U-turns around the cul-de-sac and heads away from the house. Jeanette thinks of rushing out and stopping the car. Explaining that the little girl's mother isn't home. But she freezes as her mind weighs possibilities, questions, her role in any of this. She looks out the window. The little girl stands before the neighbor's door in purple leggings and a flowered polo. She holds a pink backpack with both hands. Stares up at the door. Knocks. Stares. Knocks again. The girl scans her surroundings, and her eyes stop at Jeanette's kitchen window. They stare at each other.

———

What can she do? The cold grass crunches beneath her bare feet. A breeze comes and goes, rustles palms. The girl has a look of mild amusement or apprehension or both as Jeanette approaches, as she invites the girl into her home. The girl looks uncertain, frowns as Jeanette kneels before her.

"Just until we find your mom, okay? Do you know where she is?"

"No."

"Who dropped you off?"

"Jesse."

"Do you have Jesse's number?"

"No."

"Do you have your mom's number? Maybe a cell phone?"

"She doesn't have one. I have my number, my house number."

"How about a family member we can call?"

"No."

"No, like you don't know their number? Know their name?"

"No."

"Like an aunt or an uncle maybe? A grandma?"

"They live in El Salvador."

"Okay, well. We'll go inside. I'll fix you a little snack while we try to find your mom?"

The girl hesitates but then takes Jeanette's open hand. She lets Jeanette lead her into the house, where she lumbers onto a kitchen chair and places her backpack at her feet. Her legs dangle. She is silent, fiddles with a ruffle at the hem of her shirt.

"Do you like Hot Pockets?"

"Yes."

"Do you want a Hot Pocket?"

"Yes."

"What's your name?"

"Ana."

"Ana, I'm Jeanette."

"Is my mom dead?"

"Oh God, honey. No, she's not dead."

Monosyllables. One-word answers. The microwave beeps. Steam emerges as Jeanette cuts the Hot Pocket in two. She places a paper plate before Ana and says, "It's hot." The television announces a sale on brand-name mattresses of every kind. Prices slashed. Unbelievable savings. One-time event. Jeanette pieces together her own made-up stories: Immigration agents busted the mom for a fake social security number, some other harmless action born of necessity. The mother is desperately trying to explain that she had a daughter coming home from—

"Where were you again last night?"

Ana blows into the opening of the Hot Pocket while holding it with a paper towel. She pauses, places the pastry down.

"Jesse's."

"You slept over? Why?"

Ana regards Jeanette in a manner that makes her suddenly self-conscious. As if Ana knows something isn't right. As if Ana thinks Jeanette knows more than she's giving away. As if Ana can see right through her.

"Sometimes I sleep at Jesse's."

"Who is Jesse?"

"My babysitter."

"Will she come for you again?"

"When my mom calls and tells her to pick me up at school."

"Will she pick you up from school on Monday?"

"If my mom calls her."

Alternatively, the mother committed some kind of crime and Immigration picked her up. The mom caught a whiff that something was up and left her daughter at the baby-sitter's overnight. She's calling a relative or a friend right this moment to collect her. Someone will show up any minute now. Jeanette is embarrassed by her own problematic thoughts. Good immigrant, bad immigrant? She should know better.

"Did you say all your relatives are in El Salvador?"

"Yes."

"*All* of them?"

Ana takes a bite. She chews. She swallows.

"Yes," she says. "Can I have some juice or water, please?"

Jeanette opens her fridge. A moldy cube of cream cheese. Shredded Monterey Jack. White Cuban bread. She pours Ana a glass of tap water. Feels shame at where her own thoughts go. Does it even matter why ICE picked up her mom? Still, a child at her kitchen table. Still, awful that she never even asked her neighbor's name. She hands Ana the glass of water.

"I'll be right back. Just sit tight."

Jeanette closes the door to her bedroom. She lies back

on the bed and balances her laptop on her stomach. Google searches: *What happens to children if their parents are deported?* A link to Child Protective Services. A link to family detention centers in the region. To lawyer after lawyer after lawyer. Another search: *How to find someone detained.* An Immigration and Customs Enforcement database that requires an Alien Registration Number for the detainee. No phone number she can find. Lawyer after lawyer after lawyer. A light knock on the door. Ana has to pee. Jeanette shows her the bathroom and makes up her mind that Ana will spend the night.

In bed, Jeanette wakes, gasps, holds her breath. A sharp pain in her chest. Almost like loving Mario, wanting to run to Mario. She holds the feeling like a single bullet. No, she's gotten too far to break. Outside, a thunderstorm clicks raindrops over dying, sick banana leaves. Some nights like this— she isn't even aware of it, how her fingers find their way to her nightstand, how they search for the bottle, a healing rattle. She curls an empty fist beside her and tucks it beneath her head. Ana sleeps in the small room next to her own. Jeanette strains to listen but hears nothing.

Mario. His beard never grew in right, but he insisted on letting it grow. Red highlights streaked through his chin even though his hair had no red at all. Mario. A scar on his abdomen from a bout with appendicitis she liked to trace with her fingers. He was more organized than she but had annoying habits like forgetting wet clothes in the washing machine. He was afraid of heights.

When his parents split up, his dad went back to Argentina, started a new family in Argentina. Mario had adored him, but his dad had never called. His mother remarried, and Mario hated his stepfather, said his stepfather constantly disrespected him, and once, they'd come to blows. Mario always worried about "disrespect." He spent so much time angry over perceived "disrespect." After a fight, they liked to drive in silence to the beach, way up north, way past the tourists, to the quietest stretches of sand. Just to sit, sometimes hold hands. Mario most feared everyone in his life leaving him.

Jeanette curls on her side and places a hand to the wall as if it will pulse with an answer: what to do tomorrow, what to do every day from here on out. What color paint is this? Wonders if Ana also can't sleep.

———·———

"But how could you *do* that?" Jeanette's mother whispers across the kitchen table. The sun illuminates her face through the window, illuminates the particles of powder at her hairline. Ana watches the Disney Channel in the next room. Old Miley Cyrus bossing around a band of preteens. Laugh track. "How could you just keep someone's child overnight? Someone who you don't even know!"

Ana has been with Jeanette all morning, watching TV shows, following her around, doodling in a notebook on her belly in the spare room where she slept. Jeanette's mother got here an hour ago. She visits on Saturdays. Since leaving Mario, since detox, since rehab. She has never missed a weekend.

Jeanette's mother runs a finger over the containers before her. One holds rice and beans, the other Jeanette's favorite dessert, arroz con leche. Her mother never shows up without food she has made the night before, claiming she has made too much, that she doesn't want a refrigerator full of leftovers.

"I don't know what to do," Jeanette whispers. "I watched

Immigration officers take her mother in the middle of the night. Am I supposed to just call the cops? Will they take her to her mother? Will she go into the system?"

"It's not your responsibility."

"How can you say that?" she says. "*You're* an immigrant."

Her mother runs her tongue over her teeth and stares.

"What?" Jeanette says. "Do you ever think about how Cubans get all this special treatment, like literally you step on US ground and you have legal status. It's just so—"

"Wet foot, dry foot policy? That's going to end any day now."

"Mom, that's not even the point. Don't you think it's your *responsibility* to give a shit about other people?"

Her mother glares at her. "And what, exactly, do you think I'm doing right now?" she says. "*Giving a shit about you.*"

As a child, Jeanette used to ask her about Cuba. Her father had a whole repertoire about winding colonial streets, about the most beautiful beaches in the entire world, about the magic of sitting on the Malecón watching the waves crash. He talked about his parents, his siblings, his whole past. He drew a mythology so enchanting, Jeanette hadn't understood why her mother never said a word and would almost snap if she asked about her past. Jeanette had never even spoken to her maternal grandmother in Cuba. And even as a child, Jeanette understood that another narrative she couldn't access had shaped her life. She didn't have the vocabulary to say, *I want to know who I am, so I need to know who you've been.*

Her mother sweeps crumbs off the table into her hand. "Really, you should wipe this table every time you use it," she says.

"I do. Are you ever going to let me talk to my grand-mother? Because lately I've been thinking—"

Her mother raises her hands and shakes her head. A look Jeanette has grown accustomed to. "Call the cops. That's what they're there for. To figure this stuff out. To *help*."

"I'm just—I'm waiting to see if someone comes for Ana."

"The cops will say you kidnapped her. For all you know, there is a missing child report."

"Someone *has* to come for her. Her mother wouldn't just abandon her. She'll call the babysitter. The babysitter will say she dropped her off. Someone will come for her. I've been watching out the window. I put a note on her door. I will know when they come."

"Jeanette. This is not a game. You're on *probation*. You really want to mess everything up again?"

Her mother. Pearls, slacks, wrinkle cream, a box of blank thank-you notes. Always put together. Always carrying a whiff of her own success and composure like a cardigan at the shoulders. You look at her and just know: here is a woman with answers. So often Jeanette has wondered how she came from such a woman. So often she's felt both grat-itude and embarrassment on her behalf. Jeanette: always a woman on the verge of cracking. You look at Jeanette and think: here is a woman with stories.

Not that Jeanette's mother doesn't know loss herself. But it's a different kind of loss. Her mother lives among the Cuban elite, the First Wave, the people who lost homes and businesses and riches and ran from communism at the start of the revolution. Jeanette assumes she's like them. She can only assume. She has started writing letters to her cousin Maydelis in Cuba and new little threads have emerged: that her mother lost her father young, that her grandmother hasn't heard from her mother since she left so long ago; that she's tried but Jeanette's mother wants nothing to do with her, because of "politics," her cousin says. Maydelis has a relative with internet access at work and she called Jeanette, asked for her email. They are around the same age and had spoken on the phone periodically growing up. But online they struck an easy friendship, and she'd sparked Jeanette's curiosity, a desire to someday *go* to Cuba and meet this family she'd never known.

Jeanette suspects a deeper loss, too, one her mother won't express. Her mother laughs with abandon sometimes before catching herself, before recasting her face with dignity, poise. Jeanette suspects a different side of her mother, a smooth easiness unworn by the hard edge of new worlds, lapping at the shore of the life she abandoned. Jeanette has seen this loss in photos Maydelis has sent, photos browned with age, her mother's youthful gaze like time will never stop, like the future is an abstraction, a given. And Jeanette has wondered whether loss unspoken becomes an inherited trait.

"What are you going to tell him when he visits on Monday?" her mother says.

"My probation officer?"

Jeanette's mother smiles but her cheekbones stay in place, her skin pulls. She cups the espresso in her hands.

"Someone will come for her before then," Jeanette says. She can hear Ana giggle at the TV in the living room.

"And if they don't? It'll be the same for the girl. Whether the PO takes her Monday or the cops take her now. The only difference will be whether *you* get in trouble."

———

After her mother leaves, Jeanette and Ana walk to the park. Jeanette tapes another note to Ana's door with her phone number in case someone shows up while they are out. Hand in hand they stroll to the tiny playground: two swings, slide, seesaw, water fountain, one bench. No other children are there, so Jeanette joins Ana at the other end of the seesaw.

All day the girl's been asking questions. About her mother, where she is, when she can go home. Jeanette didn't tell her mother she'd made up a lie, that she'd said Ana's mother phoned and asked her to keep Ana for a while. *Why?* Ana wanted to know. *Why not?* Jeanette had answered. Each time Jeanette lifts her weight a little, the seesaw sends Ana floating down. Each time she sits, Jeanette hits the ground with a thud.

At night they eat take-out pizza straight out of the box, sitting cross-legged in the middle of the living room. Jeanette browses titles under Netflix's children's category. Ana wants to see none of them. Ana wants to see a "grown-up movie."

"Your mom lets you see grown-up movies?"

"It depends."

"Did you both always live here?"

"You mean next door?"

"Yeah. Or, like, in this country."

"No."

"Where did you live before?"

"El Salvador."

"When did you come here?"

"I came here twice. Once when I was a baby and last year."

"What do you mean?"

"That one."

"What?"

"I'll watch *Madagascar* even though it's for littler kids."

They watch *Madagascar*. They eat cheese sticks. Jeanette looks out the window every few hours. Jeanette waits and waits, and still nobody comes for Ana. She does the only thing that feels right: leaves the movie midway and curls up in bed, listens to the TV's drone and Ana's laugh from afar. Calls Mario. Explains nothing. Talks about the time they were both high and watched *Fantasia* in 3-D at the movie theater four times in one weekend. They laugh together. Grow sad together. Reminisce about grabbing for each other the night Mario's father died in a car accident. Honor the pain in silence. The tender feeling in the smallest action. How empty each day. How hard to stay on track. Has he . . . ? No. Has she . . . ? No. Congratulations to each other.

A pause and Jeanette says: "We never talked about having children."

"In the middle of getting high and fighting all the time? We were supposed to be like, 'Oh yeah, let's just bring another life into this and fuck that one up too'?"

"Maybe if we'd had a child. In the beginning. Maybe that would've kept us sober. Maybe that would've stopped the fighting."

She thinks Mario is crying. She hears labored breathing, shaky shuddering. She knows this routine. Knows what comes next.

"How could I have hurt you so much? I regret. So much. That I could ever have placed a hand on you."

Jeanette wants to cry, too, but is always afraid that if she lets it happen, she will never stop. That if she lets the pain seep, she will need something, someone to stop the bloodletting. Only one way to kill pain. And then the weight of it: the daily exercise, sobriety. How it drags at her feet, keeps her chained to herself.

Jeanette shakes her head no because when Mario speaks the words, then they are real. Then she is the battered ex-girlfriend, she is the fists-to-the-face that really happened.

That other life that feels so distant now. All she can feel when it's just two voices across an expanse is the knowing that still survives. The body her fingertips memorized, the universe of a relationship. All its language and borders and landscapes. A geography she studied for years and still does not understand: a man who pummels a fist into her side the same day he takes in a kitten found lying in the crook of a stairwell during a rainstorm. Nobody knows about the fights that got physical. Nobody knows these phone calls still happen. She thinks of Ana in the next room, listening to the credits. Thinks how even the best mothers in the world can't always save their daughters.

———·———

Ana wakes in the night and comes to her bed. Asks if she can sleep there instead. They lie faceup, blinking into the darkness.

"I couldn't sleep," Ana says. "I miss my mom."

"Oh, sweetie."

"When is she coming home?"

Jeanette runs her fingers through a tangle in Ana's hair. "Soon, I'm sure."

"When did she say she's coming home?"

"Oh, soon, soon." Jeanette tries to change the subject: "What did you mean when you said you came to this country twice?"

Ana turns. A small lump in the bed. A tiny cocoon. "I came when I was a baby. I don't remember. Then when I turned four, we went back to El Salvador."

"Why?"

"They made us."

"Who?"

"I don't know. The government people."

"So then you came back?"

"In a car trunk."

"What do you mean?"

Jeanette's eyes adjust to the dark. She turns, too, and can see Ana's face, brown and smooth. A little button nose. Stringy hair spread around her like a crown. She smells as children often do, a sharp, sweaty sweetness.

"We had to hide in a dark car trunk to come back. Only sometimes we could poke our heads through the back car seats to breathe."

Jeanette searches for words, thinks of the weight of Ana's story and tries to find an appropriately serious response. But Ana fidgets and yawns, seems to give the moment little importance.

"She said we had to do it for me."

"What?"

"My mom said we had to come in the back of the car trunk for me even though sometimes I miss my grandma and I had a dog in El Salvador."

"I had a dog when I was little."

"What was the dog's name?"

"Matilda."

Ana giggles and lays back. "Can you be my babysitter forever instead of Jesse?"

———·———

She knows her mother is right. She knows nobody is coming for Ana. Barefoot, she makes phone calls in the morning, T-shirt bunched at her hips, huddled in the hazy light of her room. She is not surprised to find the United States Citizenship and Immigration Services offices closed on

Sunday mornings. But she is surprised the woman who answers the ICE hotline can't find Ana's mother in the system by name and asks for an Alien Registration Number in a monotone.

"You're talking about an unaccompanied minor? Central America?"

"Well, no. The mother."

"Oh, that's good. Surge of unaccompanied minors. But if she's got a guardian, then she's probably in family detention. You got the alien minor's number?"

"No, she's—"

"Oh, well you can visit our website for more information." The silence, when the woman hangs up, is unbearable.

Jeanette finds the numbers of immigration lawyers who are much more eager to speak. They are attentive. They have questions. How is she doing? they ask. How is she holding up? It's a question Jeanette is used to. Her answer— "Fine"—is automatic.

"Oh, if only I had a dime for every mother taken away who can't contact her kid, detention guards not even listening when she says she left a kid behind," says one lawyer, whom Jeanette imagines for no reason as near retired and kind. It's the *dear*s she sprinkles: "Immigration is a civil matter, dear. It's not criminal court. There's no guaranteed phone call. There's no public attorney."

Jeanette can only squeak out an answer. Ana is at her kitchen table, drawing on blank sheets of printer paper. Jeanette has no crayons, no markers. Ana said she preferred a blue pen anyway.

"But don't you worry," the kind-voiced lawyer says. "We'll fix this even if it takes a few years."

"Years?"

"Oh, one or two. Can't imagine more than that. Prosecutorial discretion maybe. Jeanine, was it? I love that name. I'll get started right away."

And then the kind-voiced lawyer says the same thing the not-so-kind-voiced lawyers have said before Jeanette hangs up: "Bill you for the hours later, or do you want to place a credit card on file?"

It's a disappointment, maybe it's selfish, but Jeanette holds on to the word *dear* like a blip of accidental humanity caught in a stranger's throat, a version of the dust that drifts in a sunbeam that lands across her bed.

She slips into a dress. She tiptoes past the kitchen. Jeanette can hear Ana's pen scratching the paper in violent strokes. Her probation officer: he, too, will sit at her kitchen table. He, too, will scratch pen on paper. Pen on paper. It all comes down to paper.

———

Jeanette knocks on the door of the neighbor on Ana's mother's other side. "Do you know the woman who lives next door?" she says to the mustached man who holds a forty-ounce. Jeanette points toward the neighbor's house.

"All I know is she cleaned my buddy's house for twenty bucks once. Nice woman. But poor lady can't even afford a decent outfit. Damn shame, if you ask me. What with all the men might could've took care of her."

Jeanette looks down at her own outfit, at the bra straps budging from her tank top, at her dirty shoes.

Just as the mustached man is about to close the door, he pauses. "Hey," he says, pulling a phone out of his pocket. "I just remembered. You said her kid is looking for her? A friend of mine's wife is the principal at the elementary school near

here. Bet you the kid goes there. Maybe she knows something."

Jeanette stands in the street and dials the number. She
looks back at the mustached man, smiles and nods. He
watches her. And Jeanette thinks of how she wants to ask
him to shut the door but she'd never ask him to shut the
door. She doesn't ask for things she wants. Two rings and a
woman with a cigarette-husky voice answers. A dog barks in
the background. A baby cries. Jeanette attempts to explain.

"I'm sorry, *who* are you?"

"I'm . . . a member of the community. I am worried that
Immigration officers may have left a student, from your
school, behind . . . alone . . . when they took her mother."

"Oh," the woman says. "Yes, I've heard of this happening before. Have you called the police? What is the student's
name?"

The man at the door slides his thumbnail over the tab of
his beer. He looks at the nail. She can taste the beer, memory on the tongue. Why is it that men can be "hard drink-
ers"? Suave and smooth, leather and whiskey. Her father. A
woman who can't stop is simply a mess. Irresponsible.

"I—Ana," Jeanette says. She's not sure why she opts not
to tell the woman Ana's last name.

"I see," the woman says. There is a muffled sound, then
shouting: "Delilah, put the dog down! What'd I tell you
about—"

"I'm sorry to bother you—" Jeanette says, ready to end
the call. She assumes everyone wants the other person on a
call to end it.

"Ana, you said? Well, I've got near seven hundred kids
this year. I must know ten Anas. Do you have the number of
the police? I can get you the number of the police."

"I'm so sorry to bother you," Jeanette says again, and ends the call.

The man asks for her phone number as she turns to leave, and Jeanette doesn't answer but instead thinks *cleaning caddy*. She thinks *arched eyebrows* and she thinks *impossible choices* and she gets the sensation that Ana's mother already knows about her, already knows she will disappoint. She thinks *impossible choices* and she remembers, remembers so deep it hurts, why she never thought *mother* of herself. "I'm sorry," she says, and she's saying it to every mother in the world, but the man at the door doesn't understand; he is not a mother and he is just nodding.

It starts to rain as Jeanette makes her way back to the house, and she sees Ana peering out the window. For some reason the image of a tiny face through a rain-smeared window, a tiny face so full of expectation, makes her remember: She has missed her NA meeting. Jeanette stops, looks up. Will she tell her PO? He will want to know why, and he will assume it's because she doesn't want to get better, doesn't want to let go of Mario, doesn't want to see another day. She will tell him she's missed a meeting but will not miss another one, and he will be disappointed and he will not believe her, but she is used to disappointment. She is used to disbelief.

Jeanette doesn't rush back. She lets the rain patter down around her, soak through her clothes, run into her shoes. It feels good to punish herself. To stand shivering and cold in an empty street. Her sponsor told her once that the only love she knows what to do with is the kind of love that breaks a person over and over again.

Wet, squeaking through her house and leaving muddy imprints, she walks past Ana drawing still, drawing a house, drawing a bird. Jeanette takes the phone to her room. But she doesn't call Mario. She closes her eyes and tries to remember the opiate rush, the watery calm, the hit to the brain, delicious sleepy coasting. His voice in her ear: "Don't you feel every molecule that surrounds you? Everything is holding you now." She doesn't call him after she's called the cops. She doesn't call him even when the police car pulls up and she hears Ana open the door and call her name and her heart is thumping in her chest and she feels for the first time, no, *this* is what it's like to break.

3

AN ENCYCLOPEDIA OF BIRDS

Gloria
Texas, 2014

The burrowing parrot also known as the Patagonian conure also known as the burrowing parakeet is the only bird species with eyelashes. This is a little-known fact. Another little-known fact is that burrowing parrots, while often purchased as pets, become exasperated and violent if caged for too long. Burrowing parrots need interaction. They need color. If you separate two burrowing parrots, in short order the one left behind will die. She will die of loneliness.

Every day at noon we are served lunch. This is how I count the time. We don't eat with the children, because they are in classes; they eat together, at a different time. Our mud-colored trays are divided into five compartments. Today's lunch: slivers of white onion, an orange sliced into wedges, white bread (two slices), baked beans from a can. The workers are other detained women who work for three dollars a day. Everyone wants to work, so there are TVs on the wall that list the names of who will work each day and where. Two of the usual workers speak Spanish. They tell me they are sorry to see me here. They tell me, hold on. You'll be out in no time. One of them gives me my second book of bird facts. I forget how she knows I am interested in birds, but I assume I have told her. I don't remember where she got the book.

I am friends with all the women. I don't know all their names. But I know which ones have a sick child, which ones lost a husband in the desert along the way. I know whom to hug periodically, whom to gift extra rations of food. We don't speak about these—the ones who lost children, who bear wounds of rape or police torture, who are sometimes hauled screaming in the middle of the night to see one of the staff in red polo shirts. That's where we hope they are taken. They also deport people in the middle of the night. We are given no information, no answers.

Homer or Aristotle or Greek philosophers or Roman naturalists or all of them, I don't remember which, believed migrating birds were warriors. They believed migrating birds were off to do battle at the end of the earth. I imagine them whirling in a spiral toward the sky, millions of them, millions of wings, one force pulsing, beating. Powerful enough to explode into fire, that beating bird heart, to break any wall.

I don't know why I am here.

Here is for families. Here is for mostly mothers and their children. The lawyers call it family detention. The papers they won't translate call it Texas Regional Residential Center. I am alone. I don't know where my daughter is—I hope still in Florida, safe somehow, or on her way here, if safe in Florida is not an option. I pray for her every night. I pray on the concrete floor at the side of my bunk until my knees are raw and tender and I can barely stand. Some nights, my knees bleed. There is a smear of red beside my bunk. I call the smear Ana. Ana is my daughter's name. I fear I, too, am losing my mind. I don't know why I am here and I am alone and I am praying to a god I'm not sure exists but if she exists she is surely a bird, surely a migrating bird doing battle, surely she will break these walls.

———.———

Dear Ana, I am sorry. I tried to save you. Dear Ana, I am sorry. I thought I could give you a better chance. Dear Ana, I do not know if I made your life worse. I do not write any of this.

———.———

I found my first bird book in the craft room. The women can go to the craft room with their children. There are tables like the tables in the cafeteria. There are crayons, markers, yarn, paper in different colors, safety scissors, glue. There are flyers on the walls about sexual assault with bold letters spelling KEEP DETENTION SAFE! There is a bookshelf with books and puzzles on a floor made of foam. The first bird book was called *El mundo secreto de los pájaros. El mundo secreto de los pájaros* said it was for middle-grade readers. There were pictures of all the birds it described. I still come here, to the craft room, when I am saddest. I read the book on the foam floor. I read it on the foam floor and I lie on my back and I feel the foam give way beneath me. I think, how soft Ana's skin. How like bird down, her hair.

At first, I couldn't stop talking about the canyon wren of North America. The canyon wren builds a pathway to its nest with thousands of stones. Imagine it, a pebble stone path winding through the canyons, the desert, and at the end a nest full of wriggling baby birds crying out for their mother, their mother who is hopping in the distance, pebble to pebble to pebble. I am a mother. I am a pebble in the distance. Or just another person with a problem in a world too full of problems to care much about one more person behind a wall, sitting in a children's craft room, reading a children's book. I am a pebble.

After I couldn't stop talking about the canyon wren of North America, the women brought me more bird books. They asked visitors to bring them—volunteers and lawyers and, for the lucky ones, family. The women have become my bird family.

———

The playground is the happiest place in the compound but it is not like other playgrounds. The slides are gray and made of metal. The monkey bars, the tunnels—they are made of metal. The whole thing is covered by a gray plastic tarp. Like an industrial playground for robot children. Or a laboratory with double-sided mirrors where aliens play while doctors study their behavior. Still, I like to watch the children shriek and play after school or on the weekends. I don't think the children care about metal. I don't think they care about gray. Maybe some of them have no rainbow-swirled, plastic, spiraling-ladder playgrounds to compare this to.

The playground is in the courtyard, at the center of the building. The ground is concrete, or plastic grass. On one side, our bunks. On the other are the classrooms, the medical unit, the common room, and a library that has hardly any books, some computers, mostly just binders that read SELF-HELP LEGAL or KNOW YOUR RIGHTS. I browsed them once. I understood very little. Every section of the building is called a camp and labeled with an animal and a color: red bird, green frog, and so on. Nobody refers to their room that way. Nobody says they live in an animal.

There are a dozen children at the playground today. Thank God the children don't wear same-colored sweatpants and oversized shirts and can run in their full plumage. Blue shorts and red shirts and black skin and brown hair and green eyes and whirling laughter. Not all the kids are like this. Some of them sit on the concrete ledge, feet swirling sand, just watching. Some of them avoid the playground altogether and spend time trailing their mothers, the adult in them sprouting, ready to emerge in all its hardness. Ana, she is all questions and laughter. She likes to color, she likes to play soccer in the dirt, always has Band-Aids dotting her skinny legs. She likes to make up stories to pass the time. The babysitter knows her more than I. The babysitter is where she spent all her time until I finished work every night. The hurt rises, always surprising me when I least expect. I have to look away from the slide, the sand, the oil burning in the distance.

Do you think she will remember this? the woman on my left says in Spanish. We are on the bench and her child is a toddler and she is wearing yellow shorts with white daisies and she has just four front teeth. She is sitting in the sand throwing handfuls in the air while a guard stands to the side. The guard looks through her. The guard is a woman and she looks like me.

What is her name? I say.

Gladys, she says. Do you think she will remember this?

No, I lie.

I lie because I know they can detain us for months. I know this because another detained woman told me so. She is working with activists who are trying to get her out. The activists told her kids are not supposed to be detained more than twenty-one days, but the Obama administration is arguing that kids with their parents are different from kids without their parents and so the twenty-one days doesn't apply. It's all incredibly confusing. The woman has another daughter who is a US citizen. She just wants to get to her. Mothers with US citizen children have a better chance but still . . .

Which one is yours? the woman beside me says.

She is not here, I say.

What do you mean? She fidgets with her shirt.

I left my daughter with someone, I say. She was not picked up.

Then why are you here? She frowns at me.

I don't know, I answer truthfully. They transferred me from Florida. I don't know why they brought me to the family facility. I have no family with me.

You are lucky, she says. You are lucky your child will not remember this.

Your daughter won't remember this, I say. I want to hold her hand but I don't. She won't remember this, I say again.

We all know that last week, this woman and her daughter were placed in an isolation room for two days. The isolation rooms are in the medical unit. They are meant for people with TB and other such diseases, but the guards use them for punishment. The guards punished the woman after a bed raid. These raids are unannounced; they often wake us in the middle of the night, scaring the children. The guards found the woman had hidden snacks in the room. She worried because her daughter has lost so much weight since landing here. She said the isolation room smelled of antiseptic. She said the isolation room had a smiling zebra painted on the wall.

In my bunk I have started a letter to Ana. I have scratched it into the metal above me with a paper clip. It starts *Dear*

Ana, I am sorry. That's all I've written. *Dear Ana, I am sorry.*

———·———

Here is a bird fact from *Around the World in Birds: An Encyclopedia.* You can find it under the entry "Bird Suicide." In Jatinga, India, after the long monsoon months, come dark, foggy nights. On the darkest, the foggiest of these nights, hundreds of birds begin to descend the night sky, attracted to the lights below. The villagers capture them on bamboo poles. They are diving to their deaths, these mostly juvenile birds. Wildlife experts have studied the bird suicides of Jatinga, India, and they can't find a scientific explanation. I imagine myself standing in the middle of a field, a field like the one behind my childhood home in Sonsonate, in El Salvador, and I look up and there are hundreds of baby birds raining down on me: hill partridge, green pigeon, emerald dove, necklaced laughing thrush, black drongo, burrowing parrot, burrowing parrot, I am covered in birds.

I tell you this because I threw a sheet over the chicken wire fence that contains us. I didn't care if I got in trouble, but none of the guards saw. I wanted the sheet to land on the spikes, to make a softer place, a nest. I did not want a bird to kill itself. The sheet did not land over the chicken wire; it soared over the fence. For a moment, the sheet flew, and I said go. I said fly, fly, fly. Birds fly even if it kills them.

———·———

Do you have a daughter named Ana, the officer says to me in his office after I leave the playground. It is a question but he does not phrase it like a question.

Why? I say. His office has a bulletin board covered with crayon drawings made by children.

Just answer the question, he says. One of the crayon drawings is a bird. This must be a sign.

She was turned in to the authorities, the guard says. She was left behind in a house by herself after you were apprehended.

No, I say. I left her with a babysitter.

She is with the Department of Health and Human Services, the guard says. But she is an alien minor. And she is on her way here. That's why you are here.

The bird in the drawing is outlined in green crayon. The inside of the bird outline is orange. The sky is big smears of blue crayon, fat strokes. There is no sun.

No, no, no, I say. No.

I do not want my child here, where every child has a cough and the guards run their eyes over curves, hungry. I do not want my child here but I do not want her alone thousands of miles away. I want my child safe. If safe were a place, it would look nothing like any of the options, and I want to scream but I swallow, I want to claw but I smile, because I need to seem *good*. Because I need to seem worthy of something, something, some solution.

Don't worry, the man says. She's an alien too. She'll go with you.

What do you mean? I say.

She'll go to Mexico with you.

I am from El Salvador, I say. I am crying now.

To El Salvador then, he says.

What will happen to us? I say.

I think about how the orange of the bird on the wall is like the orange of my smock, my pants. How the orange could be the sun. How the bird could have swallowed the orange sun. A belly of sun.

You are in deportation proceedings, the guard answers. You know this.

So when will we go? I say. To El Salvador. When will we go?

It's a process.

But why am I here if I will go? Why am I here if I will be deported anyway?

It's a process, he says.

———|———

Beside the playground there is an open "recreation" space for the adults. Often the women will go there when the children are in school. Or sometimes a few women will take turns watching several of the children at the playground and the others will go on their own. I sit at a table with the other Salvadoran women. Beside us, another table, Guatemalans. Beside them, a table with fewer women: half Haitians and the other half I'm not sure. I think Chinese. The sun feels good on my skin after the cold of the office. Texas heat is different from Florida heat. Florida heat licks the skin. After work, I would wait for the bus that took me to the town house where I lived with Ana. I was always drenched by the time I got on the bus. I got used to the taste of sweat, licking my lips in the sun. I got used to waiting.

You look like you've been crying, says a woman named Maura. She looks so young. She has three daughters but only two are here with her.

I have been crying, I say.

She doesn't ask why. She rubs my back.

Ánimo, says another woman, Alegra, who survived a bullet to the back. She was selling vegetables at her stand when the military started shooting at protesters. Ánimo, she says. Ánimo. Be strong.

She says a woman with a baby had a court date yesterday

and they got to stay. Credible fear, Alegra says. Asylum, she says. Have you gone to the CFI prep yet? The volunteer lawyers?

CFI prep? I say.

Credible fear interview.

Credible fear? I say.

You can't say the wrong thing, Maura says. You tell the truth but it can still be the wrong thing. You can't be nervous.

I look up at the sky and think what use are words.

Texas heat is sometimes dry, like flying just above a burning house. Breathing a heat that rises, that burns the lungs. In Texas, my body is sucked dry.

Sometimes we can see oil stacks burning in the distance from this yard. When the sun sets, the Texas fields are burning in the horizon. Nobody comes to this part of Texas, nobody but oil workers and us. We must be families made of bird. If we are families that nobody wants, we will want one another. We are families made of birds and we will save one another because no one else is coming. I hug Alegra and cry again. I cry into her shoulder.

———·———

Dinner is a square of bologna, slick, a little slimy; a square of white bread, half thawed; a square of corn kernels. Water that sometimes tastes of bleach. Milk is for the children. Unlike lunch, dinner is with the children. But I am the only one who does not have a child with me, so after I finish, I offer to hold babies for some of the mothers so they can eat. I hold the babies who are too little for baby food. The babies who are still suckling on their mothers or hungrily drinking from bottles. The electric outlets are covered when not in use and none of the tables have sharp edges. There are high chairs.

This is a jail baby-proofed for babies who should not be in jail. But they will not remember, I tell myself. They will not remember, unlike Ana who is not a baby anymore or even a toddler and she will remember.

I go back to the social worker but he takes me to a blue-eyed man, a guard or a worker or the government, I don't know anymore.

You should sign this, says the blue-eyed man with a blue badge and a blue polo shirt. We are sitting on plastic chairs in a room that looks out on another room where a few people meet with family-member visitors but mostly they meet with lawyers and volunteers who visit. Sometimes they move us around, center to center. We all think they are trying to keep us as far away as possible from anyone we know. I am from Florida and I am in Texas. I knew I was going to Texas only when the officer escorted me to the American Airlines gate that said SAN ANTONIO. We are not in San Antonio. We are in some part of Texas where nobody hears us if we scream.

What is it? I say.

If you want to get out as quickly as possible, you should sign it, the blue-eyed man in the blue polo repeats. I look out the window.

In the visiting room there is a woman with a long braid down her back. She is speaking to a teenager across from her who shares her face. I imagine the woman speaking in Spanish and the teenager answering in English. I don't know if this is true. It's probably not true. They hold hands. I think of a photo I saw in a magazine on the table at a house I cleaned. *Time*. I was drawn by the photo on the cover. It was a woman, milk-coffee skin like mine, bars obstructing her face and the chalky yellow desert behind her. Tears ran down her face. She hugged a young girl through the bars. She hugged her daughter on the other side of the fence, on the US side. I wonder what does it feel like to hug someone through bars and do you look at your skin after and see the imprint, stripes down your belly, stripes on your chest? Your body, a fence.

What is it? I ask again. Do you have the form in Spanish?

No. You sign where the line is and you will leave detention faster.

Voluntary Departure, the form reads, and though I know some English, I do not know these words. There are a lot of numbers, a lot of codes. Sections 240A, 245, 248. ICE Form I-210. IJ, BIA, DHS.

What happens if I don't sign it? I ask.

Oh, the man says. They'll deport you anyways. You could stay here for who knows how long.

And what about my daughter?

These are questions for a lawyer.

I don't have one. How do I get one?

The man touches his beard and gives me a soft smile that makes me want to sink into his arms. Help me, I want to say but I don't.

The government is only required to provide a lawyer for criminal cases, says the man who does not take me in his arms. Unlawful presence of an alien in the United States is a civil issue. You can get a lawyer but you must find this lawyer on your own and pay on your own.

But all the lawyers who come here. I haven't yet had a chance to—

Look. I like you, Ms. Gloria Ramos, is it. I like you, Ms. Ramos. So I'm going to give you some advice. Sign this form. Do it for your daughter. Get yourselves out of here quickly and on with your lives.

But where do I go if I sign this? Do I go back to El Salvador?

Well, I don't know. That I don't know.

Do I see a judge and, you know, plead my case?

The man sighs. His face changes.

Listen, he says. If you want to make this harder for yourself then fine. But this is your last chance. You can sign this form and get out of here in no time or not. Up to you.

The blue-eyed man places the blue pen in front of me. I take it in my hand. *Gloria Ramos,* I sign. The man smiles again.

———

There are televisions in the common room, four of them, one in each corner. Two of them are set to children's channels and two are set to adult channels. Of the adult channels, one is always a Spanish channel. That's the one I watch every night.

When the news comes on, the guards change the channel, though sometimes we catch snippets. I think the guards don't like the Spanish news because they are always talking about immigration. They show sad graphs like border crossings down, deportations way up. They show President Obama, who likes to smile a lot. President Obama, who answers questions and some of the people asking the questions smile back and some of them don't. President Obama, who sometimes looks like he doesn't like the questions. They interview a lot of experts in fancy offices. It's bad for morale. That's what they must think.

We like the telenovelas anyways. We get the news anyways. I get it from the women who get letters from the outside where the Spanish news is not blocked. The telenovela stars are all blond and thin and rich and most of us look like the maids and witch doctors and farm peasants on the shows, but this is as close as we get to the outside, as close as we get to the life we imagined outside these walls. What would it be like? we think. What would it be like if our problem were a fight over a man or an inheritance? If the only violence we knew was killing a nemesis to steal away with her lover? Laughing, laughing. How funny to imagine this alternate universe.

In this alternate universe, maybe I wouldn't be a mother. If I am being honest, I don't always want to be a mother. Sometimes I want to be a dancer, at Salsa Rueda on Fridays at my favorite spot, the one by the Miami airport. I was learning. Sometimes I want to be a swimmer, in Key Biscayne, where the wealthy Salvadorans live, where the beach is uglier than Miami Beach but where fewer people venture so I can sink beneath the green-gray water and watch the clouds blur and no one asks anything of me. Sometimes I want to be a fighter, as when I consider attacking the men who stand guard over me. What about not caring about the consequences? Throw me in prison, beat me with your batons. Give me up to the television, another headline. Some moments I want my daughter returned to me, but God forgive me, others I want a different life for her, away from me. It is ugly to admit. But don't believe the mothers who tell you motherhood is vocation or sacrifice or beauty or anything on a greeting card. Motherhood: question mark, a constant calculation of what-if. What if we just gave up?

There's no bedtime, technically, but we can't roam after ten o'clock. It's not jail. That's what the guards say constantly: It's not jail, be glad it's not jail. Most of us go to sleep early because the children have school the next day plus we have nothing better to do. My room has five bunk beds lining the walls with identical blue plastic mattresses. Below the bunks are plastic bins in which to store our things. Most of us don't have *things*. There is one plastic table painted over with a checkerboard and backgammon. We don't play. There are no pieces to play with, plus none of us know the rules. There is a door that does not lock and Plexiglas windows with chicken wire. Sometimes a child cries at night but is not allowed to sleep with the mother; the guards will come in the middle of the night and break it up. There are too many people here. That's another thing the guards tell us. They complain that there are too many people and not enough guards and they're building another place like this not far from here but it is taking too long. The guards complain about it together but we hear it and we tell one another: There are too many people here. We tell each other: This must mean they'll let us out sooner. Because it seems logical that they'll let us out sooner if there are too many people. Some of us even beg, Just deport me already.

I don't say this. At least we are safer here. I fled the person who killed my brother. Simmering violence. A government whose response was to militarize the streets. Of course with US help. Of course they don't talk about this on the news. I'm afraid of the conditions that create violence. I'm afraid of the police. I'm afraid of the army. I'm afraid of how I survive in a country where the official currency is the US dollar and farmers can barely afford the abono for the milpas but the rich hire private security firms. I'm afraid every moment of every day, thinking about my life here, thinking about my life if it's not here, thinking about Ana, thinking about my people, my beautiful people, so many young people dying in the streets. Parents sending their children off into the unknown, thinking maybe they won't make it to the United States but maybe they will. Maybe they will and if they stay here maybe they won't. I know all this because the women who get letters or make calls ask about my town for me, women who have sisters or uncles or cousins from all over Sonsonate. Most of the women crossed not long ago. Border Patrol holding cells where they crank the AC, from the hielera to here. If they force me back, we will have to find a new place that is safer, Ana and I. But where, with what, how? I turn on the sticky, sweaty mattress to face the wall and think, What kind of fear is credible? There are so many kinds of fear. I don't like that the rooms won't lock.

———•———

Some mornings, I wake up really early. I wake up at six and head to the common room before anyone else gets there. I like to put in the National Geographic DVD another woman gave me. I've watched it so many times. It is in English but I can make out some of what the deep-voiced narrator says. I can enjoy the bursts of feather and branch and leaf and sky. I watch it all the way through until my favorite part. The camera zooms in and I see them: the hoatzin chicks.

Hoatzin chicks differ from their parents. When young, hoatzins have two claws on each wing. The claws go away once the chicks mature into adults, but as children they can climb trees with their wing claws, jump into water and claw themselves out, fight predators if they need to. They are beautiful birds, the hoatzin, my favorite of all the birds. They have bloodred irises crowned by sea-blue plumage. They have red crests that rise up like crowns. This is how I picture my daughter, flying through these gates to me, shedding handcuffs and perplexing Immigration officers as she expands her wings and flaps them viciously, as she rises past the walls, past the chicken wire, past the guard booth. This is how I see her coming to me, arms spread, sun in her belly, royalty made of delicate bone and feather and laughter. My daughter, knowing she is royalty and ready to spread her killer claws.

4

HARDER GIRL

Jeanette
Miami, 2002

Johnson's lips were rubber clams. His breath was stale and hot, though the sand pricked cold against Jeanette's back. She turned her head when he tried to kiss her again, as if by looking away, nothing was happening, nothing but the ocean at her side. It's never really dark in Miami Beach, even on a moonless night. Ocean Drive dripped its neon across a dying street, across a concrete wall, over sand dunes, all the way to shore. Eerie exit-sign green, Barbie-doll pink: they were awash in the palate of a night all wrong.

Jeanette spotted the hand first. Bloated, palm up, on the wet sand. Skin purple-red like a heart carved out of the body. She cheered it on, even. *Yes, my little heart, run to sea and leave this moment.* Then she followed the lines and angles, and a fuller graph appeared: an arm as the water receded, bobbing breasts as the water rushed back.

"Holy *fuck*," she whispered. Shock gave her strength she couldn't muster a moment before. Jeanette dug her heels into the sand and pushed Johnson off.

He tumbled onto his side, onto his elbow. "What the fuck?" He followed her gaze: water receding, body. "Fuck!"

They scrambled to their feet. Jeanette's tank top was bunched under her armpits. Her nipples poked through a mesh purple bra. She pulled her top down and her denim shorts up from her ankles. They stepped closer to the water's edge but stopped before the body like an invisible perimeter held them back.

Johnson said the obvious. Something like, "Holy shit. It's a dead body." The body was of a woman, perhaps in her forties, perhaps in her sixties. It was impossible to tell.

"What do we do?" she managed.

The dead woman's eyes were open, the pupils fixed on some faraway horizon. They were milky, looked like they'd be pebble hard to the touch, and the mouth was slightly parted like death had come as she said something innocuous. *How's the weather over there?* mouth barely closing over *ere*.

"Fuck, I don't know. Fuck! I'm so high. Okay, give me a moment. I need to think. Give me a moment." Johnson ran a hand through the wisps of hair left on his almost-bald head.

A moment ago Jeanette had thought she'd reached the precipice of who she wanted to be, thought she'd finally walk the halls of Gables High like a harder girl, like the ones with boyfriends who didn't have to lie about sexual experience. They'd always both intrigued and frightened her. She knew they knew of things she only read about in romance paperbacks with worn spines or watched on HBO late at night with the volume muted so her parents wouldn't hear. She believed the harder girls, the cooler girls, were contagious and she, dripping with want, could siphon their cool. She'd tried to move in their orbit, hoped they'd see her as one of their own. But until this night, she had lived with fear they'd find her out for the girl she really was.

Now she was standing in front of a dead body and knew of things none of the cool girls would ever know.

————

It started like this: Two girls in denim coochie-cutters hanging outside a gas station. Sasha's car was parked in an IHOP lot. They'd just finished eating a stack of pancakes for dinner. They were bored. Sasha's mom was at her boyfriend's place in West Palm Beach, where she spent most weekends. Jeanette's mother was home recovering from a tummy tuck. Her father was home drunk.

They'd split a joint and hot-boxed Sasha's car at the car wash. They did that often: selected a deluxe super-plus wash, which meant the car went in and they didn't have to pull out for like fifteen minutes. So nice, to be pulled along, car moving on its own, no decisions. In a haze of smoke, Jeanette had watched automatic rollers paint Sasha's windshield with giant, clumsy, felt-robot hands. The robot and Jeanette had blown hot air at each other. Then, giggling, they'd rolled into the sunshine, opening the windows to air the car as a bored young worker took Sasha's money and shook his head in disbelief and, probably, a bit of jealousy. Then IHOP. Then they'd wanted cigarettes. That's why they went to the gas station.

Jeanette and Sasha had a routine. They stood off to the side, by the quarter air pumps, out of the sight line of whoever manned the cash register inside the shop. They watched for the right kind of guy getting out of his car. The best bets were guys over thirty, without girlfriends or wives or kids in the car. Jeanette was better at asking than Sasha. She'd never said it to Sasha's face, of course, but Jeanette knew it was because she was prettier. Sasha, with her small chest and habit of wearing headbands, looked younger. The only guys who eyed Sasha at the gas station were the really old ones and they had agreed to draw the line at sixty. Old, old guys were creepy.

That Saturday, Jeanette had tried one guy before Johnson. The guy had been in his thirties maybe, with a crew cut and a tattoo of Florida that said GOD BLESS THE GUN-SHINE STATE in Old English letters below. She was sure he'd buy them a pack. But he'd brushed Jeanette aside with laughter while scanning her body and lifting the gas pump from its holster.

"Sweetie, I'm on parole, and you aren't worth it," he'd said.

She was mortified. So she tried extra-hard with the next guy, with Johnson: adjusted her bra so extra cleavage spilled over her orange top, sucked her stomach in, reapplied strawberry Lip Smackers and a light-brown lip liner. She'd dabbed some CK One between her boobs.

Johnson pulled up in a beat-up bloodred Toyota. He looked like a dad, or like one of Sasha's mother's boyfriends, in camouflage shorts and a white T-shirt that read TONY'S TACKLE AND BAIT SHOP in faded blue. He had green eyes and acne scars, muscular arms that strained his shirtsleeves. The Toyota had dark-tinted windows.

Jeanette chewed her gum as she walked up to him. She smiled her most pleasant smile, the kind her dad liked. *Smile, it's your best feature,* he'd say to her as she left the house for school each morning.

Johnson looked up with his wallet in his hand. Sweat beaded on his forehead. She said hello, and he sized her up, didn't return her smile.

"I was wondering . . ." Jeanette chewed her bottom lip and looked toward the shop door. A laminate tacked to the glass read EMPLOYEES DO NOT HAVE ACCESS TO SAFE.

"Me and my friend"—she motioned toward Sasha with

her chin—"we want to buy cigarettes but we forgot our IDs. If I give you the money, would you buy us a pack of Marlboro menthols? The green pack?" She held out a crumpled twenty, gave her best smile again.

Johnson squinted. "How old are you?"

"Eighteen."

He frowned and cocked his head, softened into a smile. "What if I don't want your money? What if I do it as a favor?"

The night was sticky and Johnson's hand left a moist imprint on his wallet. His eyes were on Jeanette's chest and she knew she had him. She brought her arms closer together. The cross of her gold chain disappeared between mounds of flesh.

"You don't have to do that," she said.

It was uncomfortable enough to ask for cigarettes; Jeanette didn't know how to accept additional favors. She glanced toward Sasha but Sasha chewed a fingernail, not paying attention.

"It'd be my pleasure," Johnson said. "Maybe you can pay me some other way."

Jeanette wasn't stupid. She got it right away. *Oh,* went a flick in her head. She knew when wanting her became *wanting her.* Usually it scared her a little, men's comments. She'd walk down Kendall Drive by Sasha's house, a street that felt more like a congested highway, and men would honk at her, would follow them, would stop to gawk and shout. She liked it. She hated it. Thought it was a fact of life, like waiting for the light to change or taking an umbrella just in case.

But she pictured the men following through on their promises, shoving her into their cars, to *fuck* her, to *fuck* that *juicy ass.* That's what those cooler, harder girls did, wasn't it? They got fucked. But she couldn't picture the popular boys at school, boys like Chris and Raul and Marcelo, talking to their girlfriends like that, expressing such raw desire. She was amazed she could inspire such want, such need. She was baffled that these same men who shouted at her and Sasha did things that, say, her mother and father did. She could not picture her father *fucking* her mother. She thought, *These men must want me more than anyone wants my mother, more than anyone wants the coolest girl in school.* Then she felt good.

So she smiled some more at Johnson. Pretended she didn't understand. "What kind of favor?" she said.

Johnson laughed. He looked around. He was the kind of guy who couldn't stop looking around as if his next words were on cue cards scattered in the distance.

"What are you girls doing tonight? You know, after you smoke your cigarettes?"

Jeanette wondered what he wanted. She wondered if men who wanted to fuck her would accept a night driving around the city. She saw dirt under Johnson's fingernails and wondered if he was the kind of man who built things or tore them apart, who knew about machines in a way her own father did not.

"We don't have any plans," Jeanette said.

The man nodded. "I see."

Johnson looked at a cue card on the left, a cue card on the right, then opened his door to grab something from the passenger side seat. He handed her a flyer.

On the flyer was a woman in a silver metallic bikini, oil-shiny, hair cascading around her shoulders. The woman's lips were slightly parted. The woman was so happy to be on the front of a flyer. She wanted to get *fucked*.

TMS Productionz presents Wet n Wild, the flyer read.

"What is this?" Jeanette said.

Johnson watched Jeanette watch the flyer. "You ever been to a foam party, sweetie?" he said. "This one starts in an hour. Lasts all night."

All night, all ages, read the flyer. *No Cover for Ladies.* Little cutout faces of five men surrounded the woman in the bikini whose hard breasts shone like apples the size of their heads. They were the faces of various DJs—DJ Ztar Ztruck, DJ Taz, DJ Juicy J. Bubbles floated like halos around their heads.

"Let me ask my friend," Jeanette said.

———·———

Sasha and Jeanette had their first fight. Sasha said no, absolutely not, she would not go anywhere with a man she didn't know. This had angered Jeanette. Something was finally happening to them. Something besides getting high at the car wash and eating pancakes. Something was happening to Jeanette besides her father naked and sweaty passed out on the couch and her mother carefully reapplying mascara after crying and dabbing vanilla-scented lotion between her breasts because, she said, every woman should have a "signature scent." Something was finally happening that didn't feature a predictable ending. Jeanette didn't understand how someone like Sasha, who went skydiving once and drove high without her seat belt, had never considered testing what lay on the other side of men in cars who wanted them.

"I'm going whether or not you go with me," Jeanette said to her, and knew in that instant that Sasha was pretending even more than she was, that Jeanette was harder and floating closer to the girls they both thought they were.

"I'm not bailing you out if you get stuck in South Beach or something," Sasha said to her. Jeanette heard the door jingle. Johnson walked out of the 7-Eleven and waved a pack of Marlboros at them, smiling. "And you can keep the stupid cigarettes."

"Fine, go home, and I'll tell you all about the party tomorrow," said Jeanette. "I thought you were supposed to be my best friend."

"This is so stupid," Sasha said, already walking toward the IHOP parking lot. Jeanette let herself wonder for a moment how bad Sasha would feel if they found Jeanette's body the next day, maybe at the bottom of some lake or worse. She couldn't let herself think of *worse*. Excitement rippled through her, and fear. Two emotions too similar to tell apart most days.

Fear was her father drunk.

But this didn't feel like that. This felt like growing up.

Jeanette's mother had tried to talk to her about sex once. She'd found a condom in Jeanette's purse. Her mother had tried to borrow her purse without even asking, which had angered her. It was a vintage quilted Chanel, her father's gift to her on her thirteenth birthday. Her father gifted his love, her father who never bought her mother anything. Jeanette sensed an attempt at reclamation when her mother borrowed her purse without asking.

Jeanette liked that her mother thought boys were fucking her when she found the condom at the bottom of the Chanel bag. The truth was that she had been flirting with Manny, one of the popular boys, one of the boys who would flunk out in a year, who sat next to her in chemistry and copied her answers. She was good at chemistry.

"Do you like it raw?" Manny had said to her in class one day. Jeanette had no idea what he meant, though now she knew. But she had feigned knowledge because she liked that Manny thought she was the kind of girl who'd know. She liked that Manny pinched her waist and winked when he said it.

"Yeah," she said, popping her gum and shrugging.

"Damn, girl. Me too," said Manny. "Guess neither of us needs this then." He handed her the condom and cracked up in laughter.

The teacher scolded them both, and the pathetic girls, the ones nobody wanted, looked toward them with disgust. Jeanette kept the condom and placed it in every purse or backpack she used each day or night, a reminder that she was wanted. And she pictured that when it finally happened, the fucking, she'd pull it out and the guy doing the fucking would know that other people wanted her too.

"Look, I'm not going to pretend I can stop you from, you know, doing . . . you know . . . ," her mother had said, refusing to meet Jeanette's eyes. "I just want you to know that nobody is going to want you—for serious things, things like marriage—if you are, you know, if you've been, well, if you've been *used* already."

Jeanette had giggled. Nobody looked more used up than her mother. She'd never have said it to her, but Jeanette knew her mother was just jealous her father didn't want to use her anymore. That nobody wanted to use her mother. That her mother was *useless*.

On the car ride to South Beach, Johnson told Jeanette his name was Johnson. Jeanette was embarrassed she hadn't thought to ask. She didn't give her real name. She told Johnson her name was Caro. Caro was the hottest, most popular girl at school. Caro was Manny's girlfriend the year before, which meant Caro liked it raw.

"How old are you *really*, though?" Johnson said, switching the manual gear up a level and getting on the highway.

"You know what? Don't answer that. I'm barely legal myself, ha ha ha."

Jeanette didn't get it. She was so tired of pretending to get things. She switched the subject. "I've been to a club before."

"Oh yeah?"

Johnson had the radio station tuned to Power 96. Jeanette thought he looked too old to listen to hip-hop but then realized she just thought that because her parents never listened to Power 96, only the easy listening station and Spanish talk radio, what she assumed all adults over a certain age listened to.

"Yeah. In South Beach. Got super drunk. It was so fun."

This wasn't a lie. Two months earlier she'd used Sasha's sister's ID, and even though the two of them looked only slightly similar, the bouncer at Club Tigre had glanced at her rhinestone bra top and slid open the velvet rope. She remembered dancing on a table. She remembered older guy after older guy buying her drinks. She remembered Sasha's attachable ponytail that made Sasha's hair longer and thicker. She remembered vomiting on the side of the road on their way home.

"Well, it'll be fun tonight. You ever been to a foam party?"

"Yeah," Jeanette lied.

After an uncomfortable pause she said, "So what do you do?" This was what grown people said to each other according to all movies and TV shows. They were passing the downtown skyline, which meant Miami Beach was minutes away. Select windows of high-rises lit up like those Lite-Brite toys from when she was young. She pictured reaching out and plucking each window into her palm so the whole city went dark.

Johnson eyed her before returning his eyes to the road. "Are you some kind of hooker?"

"What?"

"What's your endgame here? I'm not giving you money. What are you trying to do to me?"

"Fine," Jeanette said, measuring the depth of her next lie. "I'll tell you. I'm seventeen and a half." She thought that's what he wanted to hear. She thought that would set him at ease.

But Johnson just frowned at her. "I don't get it," he said.

They drove in silence until they crossed the bridge to the beach. Immediately the human landscape changed. Women in stilettos. Men in suits. Sex and sexiness pouring from every crevice.

But the club was nothing like she'd expected. They'd passed the places with long lines and thin women checking names off clipboards. They'd passed the hotel lobbies lined with bored valets watching over expensive cars. Their club was in an alley off Ocean Drive that smelled like piss and mildew. There was no line, no velvet rope. There was one skinny guy with red eyes who didn't bother to ask her for ID, which would have blown Jeanette's cover. He gave them both orange wristbands.

Inside there were only a few people. More men than women. A handful who looked like high schoolers just like her. The space was one small black rectangle with a hose-like contraption blowing bubble foam that reached to Jeanette's waist. A disco light circled in a frenzy. *Get ur freak on*, Missy advised. *And if you want me, want me . . . come on, get me now*—An air horn interrupted.

But Jeanette didn't act surprised. She asked Johnson for a drink and he obliged. She asked for an amaretto sour, which Sasha had told her about at the first club, but he came back with something called a Long Island iced tea.

"With Bacardi 151!" he shouted over the music into her ear. "Let's see what you're made of. We're gonna have fun tonight, little girl."

She downed the ice tea quickly to impress him. He seemed impressed. He bought her another one. Jeanette wondered how many drinks she could get away with. She was mesmerized by this newfound power. Men wanting to buy her things just like her father did. She felt like Queen Caro, ruler of all the men, floating in her foam kingdom, watching women in bikinis grinding against men with their shirts around their necks. She liked the way they danced like they also knew their power. But how could she compete? How could she show Johnson she was even more desirable?

She felt woozy from the drinks. She decided to up her game. She bent over and dipped her hands into the foam. It was like reaching into a cloud. She felt her shorts rise up over her butt cheeks. She pictured Johnson wanting her butt cheeks. She backed up into him.

But he didn't seem surprised. He just grabbed her waist and jerked it back harder. He had a drink in his hand and he tipped it over and a stream of liquid rolled down Jeanette's back and into her hair and then into her ears and then into her nose.

She shook her head but felt dizzy. She stood up again.

"You little freak," Johnson yelled into her ear. He pulled a spliff and a lighter out of his back pocket and lit up. He handed it to Jeanette. She noticed two guys beside them watching her. She puckered her lips when she sucked the spliff and stared one of them in the eye.

Johnson was sweaty. Wet orbits sprouted from his armpits. His car had smelled like cigarettes and perspiration, and now he smelled like his car. He was nothing like her father. Jeanette's father was a drunk, but Jeanette's father was a *neat* drunk. She danced a circle around Johnson, gyrating her pelvis. Her father went to work in a suit and changed into his surgical scrubs at the hospital. He always smelled of Listerine and rubbing alcohol. She put her hands on her knees and made circles with her ass. He'd only touched her once when he was drunk.

Johnson grabbed a handful of her ass and slid a finger along the seam of her jeans. That made her straighten. She couldn't explain why she felt different all of a sudden. Nothing had changed. She couldn't explain why Johnson kind of disgusted her—in a bad way—now. She wanted to go home. She was so dizzy. Jeanette sat down on a foam-wet plastic chair and felt her shorts saturate.

She pictured what the place would look like with muted sound—all those bodies in ridiculous movement, all those men eyeing convulsing bodies, perspiring, breathing heavy. The one bartender, a woman in a black bustier, looked like she watched the scene with muted sound. She was the only one who saw how funny it all was. Jeanette wanted to kiss her, the only real person left.

Johnson motioned with his chin and grabbed her arm. He dragged her to a corner by the bathrooms. Every wall was a mirror. The tiny space looked like a kaleidoscope and Jeanette smiled thinking of herself as a piece of colored glass that morphed, shifted into different patterns. *I'm a star. I'm a Magic Eye. I'm nothing at all.*

Johnson took a small baggie of white powder and a key chain with three keys out of his back pocket. He dipped a key into the baggie like he was collecting a teaspoon of sugar. Then he brought the key up to his nose in one quick swoop, snorted deeply, and threw his head back. He shook his head like a wet dog.

"God damn!"

Jeanette had never seen anyone do coke. She didn't know anyone at her high school who even spoke about coke. She had always assumed cocaine was one of the *drug addict* drugs, like heroin in a syringe, the kind of drug nobody in her circles would ever do. The kind that existed so her drugs—weed, an occasional ecstasy roll or some bars from someone's mom's prescription—didn't count as *real* drugs.

"Take a bump," Johnson said to her, dipping the key again and holding it up to Jeanette's face.

She was afraid, and he still disgusted her. But she was even more afraid of what would happen if Johnson discovered she wasn't the kind of girl he thought she was. What kind of humiliation would rain down on her, whether he'd dump her on her doorstep like a child and nothing would have really changed in her life that night. The only thing that could make her harder than the hard girls was if she did things even they wouldn't do. Jeanette was getting dizzier and dizzier. She felt nauseated.

"You've never done this, have you?" Johnson said to her, eyes suddenly all pupil, fried eggs with black yolks.

Jeanette didn't say anything.

"Just snort it really, really deep, like you're trying to breathe all the way into your skull."

Jeanette took the key and snorted as Johnson had. She thrust her head back like him, like this was an action she'd repeated so many times it'd become automatic.

The snorting felt like drowning. It felt like breathing in water accidentally when she chicken-fought in the pool with friends, a burning all up her face and then a metallic drip at the back of her throat. She had a taste in her mouth like she'd swallowed blood.

"Good little girl," Johnson said, giving her ass a squeeze.

He took the key in his hand and shoved the tip into Jeanette's mouth. "Now run this on your gums like a good girl. Lick that key clean."

Jeanette did as she was told, more metal in the mouth. More blood. She felt part of her mouth go numb.

The high came so fast, Jeanette wasn't sure it was really a high and not some kind of trick of the mind. Her body felt electrified and the dizziness evaporated. She was seized by an excitement, the feeling of something incredible about to happen. She felt at the precipice of a whole new life and couldn't believe she'd ever doubted herself. She was amazing! Queen Caro times infinity squared, ruler of all the dance floor, killer of all the men. What would it feel like if she turned the tables on Johnson? If she ended up chopping his body into pieces so everyone he'd ever known would grumble, *What was he thinking, letting a stranger into his car who could have been a serial killer for all he knew?*

"Let's dance," she said, unable to get the words out fast enough.

Johnson wore an exaggerated smile like a marionette. He sweated even more. Jeanette just wanted to dance dance dance. She just wanted to kill him kill him kill him. That was the solution! How had she missed it all this time? The next time her father came at her drunk, wanting a too-tight hug, the next time he had an angry outburst, she'd simply kill him. How simple. The music split into individual notes. That was the weed high bleeding into the coke high, she imagined. She could suddenly identify every instrument, every tempo change, every beat, every lyric. The music became physical like gas into water; if you had asked her at that moment what each music note tasted like, she'd have been able to answer.

They danced but it wasn't about sex anymore. It was about

the miracle of having a body. The miracle of not understanding a single thing about firing neurons, about the mechanics of moving her ass, but doing it anyway. She danced to *I don't think you're ready for this jelly!* She screamed, *For the mamis and the señoritas, Cuban girls and fine Boricuas!* She twirled and thought, *U remind me of a girl I once knew . . .*

It was three in the morning when they left the club. Jeanette had her cell phone but nobody had called. She imagined her mother puffy from the surgery, fuzzy on whatever painkillers the plastic surgeon had given her. Asleep. She probably wouldn't notice how late Jeanette got home.

The high had started to fade. Now Jeanette felt panicky, watching the euphoria leak out of her, desperate with the knowledge that her confidence hadn't been real, just a chemical trick. She couldn't remember where Johnson had parked but he was leading her by the arm toward the ocean, they were crossing the boulevard toward the dunes.

"Where are you taking me?"

Johnson also seemed depleted. He seemed angry now. At the club, he'd stopped dancing and nearly punched a guy who looked at Jeanette from head to toe. A bouncer had intervened, and Johnson said they were leaving.

"Let's go look at the water," he said, not even turning to see Jeanette as he led her by the arm.

"Why?"

He didn't answer. Jeanette was so tired. She just wanted to go home.

The beach was dark enough that no one would see them unless they walked down the stairs toward the shore and right up to them. But it wasn't so dark that she couldn't see Johnson's eyes. The Miami Beach skyline formed a lighted wreath around them. Jeanette took a breath of salt air and felt the airy rumble of a wave. *Okay, do what you're going to do*. The water shone black, pure black, the boats in the distance shiny bobbing dots when he held her down.

It was the dead body that saved her. Later, she would think of this moment and know that nothing else would have stopped Johnson's hands digging all over her skin and into her brain, implanting the sound of skin on skin that she'd retrieve with shame the rest of her life. Later, standing on the shore, watching water bob around the lifeless woman, only then would she feel a deep sorrow for this body that saved her own.

"I'll call the cops. About the body," she said, and Johnson responded, "You crazy? We're high as fuck. You're like twelve years old. Shit. Shit."

"I'm fifteen!" she said.

At their right a locked pile of beach recliners wrapped in metal twine leaned precariously. An empty lifeguard booth cast shadows over its dirty plastic bands.

"Jesus Christ," Johnson yelled at her. "Jesus Christ. Jail time—that's what it fucking is."

Jeanette stared at the tower of beach loungers. She wanted to climb its rungs and go to sleep on top, a disgraced version of the princess and the pea.

"Well, we can't just leave her here," she said. "Can we just leave her here?"

Jeanette wasn't used to a grown man without an answer. The world felt so much more dangerous, so much more uncertain than it had just a day ago. Tendrils of the dead woman's hair pulsed like jellyfish with the tide. She had hair the color of Jeanette's, hair the color of her mother's.

Johnson had cast off his sneakers earlier, and his socked feet left little oval nests in the wet sand along the shore as he paced. Jeanette placed a foot in one of the little foot pools and marveled at the empty space.

"We gotta go," Johnson said, grabbing her by the arm and pushing her toward his shoes and damp T-shirt that lay in a pile. "Come on. Get yourself together."

"What about—?"

"They'll find it. Someone will find the body in the morning."

Johnson sprinted toward Ocean Drive, holding his pants up and wobbling like a duck. Jeanette followed, thinking their footprints that led up to the body were a bad idea. She wondered if she could call the cops from the car. But how would she explain why they had fled? Why she'd been at the beach after dark in the first place?

The street was empty, illuminated by the glow of art deco hotel fronts like the whole place was as real as a lit-up plastic Christmas tree. They ran two blocks inland, a few trickles of bleary-eyed clubbers meeting their path, unimpressed by their half-dressed, panicky race toward nowhere. They ran past closed tourist shops full of mannequins, balloon-breasted women in bikinis, blank-faced men in silly T-shirts that said things like FBI: FEMALE BODY INSPECTOR. Rows of shot glasses, crystal dolphins, bleached sand dollars. Johnson with a hand holding his pants up, Johnson running with the wobble of a toddler taking its first clumsy steps.

It had happened like this: Johnson thrusting her into the sand and pinning her by the shoulders. Like this: a tiny crab scurrying inches from Jeanette's sideways-turned head, minute legs like fingers running over a piano. She didn't yell or protest. She didn't say no. She felt the futility of language, that it couldn't capture the knowledge that what was happening was exactly what she'd expected could happen, that she was disappointed that once again the unexpected hadn't won out. That strange men in cars were exactly what everyone had warned they were. That sex was just sex and not something that would clean her from the inside out, deliver her new to the world.

As Johnson undid her shorts, as he tugged at her tank top, she wanted to yell that he should stop—not because she wanted him to but because why would *he* want to be exactly what everyone expected? Didn't he know how exhausting it was? She couldn't find her voice, but it didn't matter. Jeanette knew it then: harder girls weren't happy. Probably, nobody was.

Jeanette followed until she didn't. She followed until Johnson no longer looked back. Then she stopped along an empty street and curled onto a bench. She wondered if Johnson would come back looking for her. She wondered what a sunrise would look like on this particular street, what a body would look like coming into the light.

5

FIND YOUR WAY HOME

Gloria
Mexico, 2016

When you first got there, to the detention center, I was afraid you would forget: the feel of bathwater (that feeling of calming suspension, like in a womb!), the way Miami smells of salt, what it feels like to run for miles and never hit a wall or fence. I was afraid captivity would shape you into something new and unrecognizable. I was afraid I would bear witness to a turning point, look back and think, *That was the moment that shaped your life into disaster,* or worse, *I was the one who caused disaster.*

But you were resilient, and I guess it's no surprise. I've watched mewling kittens fight for life, the mother flattened into bone and fur by a careless car, and why should a human child be any different? I like to think you need me but I know now—that the feeling is more about my own survival than yours.

When you first got there, I wasn't moved to another room. Our room had already swelled with more people than beds even though they said that wasn't allowed. So you slept on the plastic cot with the scratchy blanket with me, and we both tried to will ourselves smaller to make space for the other. You asked me only once where we were and why. I told you it was only temporary, but by then, weeks had passed. You seemed to sense my struggle to answer so you stopped asking. But I could see you swallow the question and it pained me.

You didn't like your new "school." You complained that you were in the second grade but had to take a class with first graders and kindergarteners. You called them babies and I wanted you to stop growing, to remain in this moment. You said some of the kids couldn't speak English but that when you tried to speak to them in Spanish, the teacher said you weren't allowed. You complained that you already knew everything they tried to teach you. I was miserable and proud at the same time.

You didn't like the food either but this was easier to get used to. It was hard, watching you no longer savor, lose that pleasure. I watched how eating became mundane. But there were bigger losses to mourn. I couldn't think about food.

It's funny, how a place can look so different when you crop the edges. I'd watch you play with the other kids in the industrial-looking playground, all that laughter, all that running and jumping. Except for the wall and chicken wire looming beyond, this could be any multicultural playground in any multicultural city full of happy, thriving kids. It reminded me of when I was young, long before you, in Sonsonate. A group of Christian missionaries came to our town and they built a school and a church. We watched them from behind our porches and favorite trees, how they delighted in everything we eschewed, favored the grubbiest clothes and the simplest food despite the rolls of bills in their lanyard wallets.

One day, as I played with two school friends, one of the

Christian missionaries approached and spoke in Spanish to me. "Despite having so little," she said, "you are so happy. You could teach the children in my country so much about what's really important in life."

I hadn't known until that moment that I had so little. Even as an adult, when I had experienced enough to place my own life in comparison, I marveled at the woman's comment. I wondered what she had expected: sad poor people being sad and poor at every sad, poor moment of their lives? She mistook happiness for what it was—how we survive and build lives out of the strings we hold. But she must have known, deep down, that she was lying to herself. She had said I knew the secret, what was really important in life, what made a person happy. If that was true, it didn't make sense when she went back home and left all that "happiness" behind.

What I am trying to say is that we told jokes back then, at the detention center. We laughed in our little cot until the other women shushed us. We told jokes about our situation that were funny enough to muffle the dread inside.

Almost a month. That's how long you laughed in an industrial playground, how long you sat bored in a class full of "babies," how long you forgot the taste of your mother's cooking. You can count yourself lucky because on the television now they talk about all these kids locked up in cages. Like it wasn't bad enough they separated adult family members, sent them to opposite sides of the country. I didn't think it could get worse. You have childhood memories that are not policed by a guard standing just off the frame. For this, I am grateful.

I don't know what you remember, but they didn't tell us where they were taking us. I thought we were going before a judge finally. I thought I could argue my case, my credible fear. I had practiced. Instead they boarded us onto a bus with bars on the windows and dropped us off in Mexico. We were Salvadoran by nationality but Mexico was just a few hours away, and that's where we'd come from, so there they left us. Said, *Find your way home.* We were supposed to be turned over to Mexican immigration officials, but I guess they didn't show up. Or they thought we were Mexican. It was all very disorganized. I don't know how to reach the nuns of the center for deported migrants that fed us that night and gave us a place to sleep beside all the other dazed faces. If I could reach them, I would say simply: Thank you. If only for one night, you kept us safe.

There are three choices for people like us in Mexico. We make our way back across the border and risk even harsher punishment if we are caught, because then we are "repeat offenders," for us, a second time. We make our way back to our original homes, places we fled once because hunger shadowed, death shadowed. Or we stay with the others like us here, a hard choice too: here, where we'll be chased and harassed, cash out for yet another outstretched hand in uniform to escape yet another van to yet another unknown. And I just kept thinking of how much harder crossing had become, kept thinking of all those bodies turned skeleton in the desert, all those bodies stacked atop one another in the morgues; so many bodies, too many bodies. Bodies washed ashore. Names we'd never know.

I opted for the last choice, to stay in Mexico, and I hope you will understand someday why I did so.

I know it was hard for you. You couldn't even write in Spanish since you'd spent nearly all your life studying in English. The water made you sick because your stomach wasn't used to it. You cried for your old life every day. You begged to go back to Florida and how could I explain it to you, you so small and full of hope still? That the place you called home had never considered you hers, had always held you at arm's length like an ugly reflection?

I realize someday you may ask why we embarked on any of this in the first place, why I didn't keep you breathing mountain air in your first home, water the color of a peacock feather, the sound of a guitar in a cathedral plaza, why I didn't keep you in a place that never called you foreign. I guess the time has come to tell you about my pregnancy, though I have avoided it all these years.

I don't know his name, Ana. I don't even know his face. I remember, most, his hands, cracked and dry. How his nails were long and underlined with muck. How he tasted of stale smoke, smelled of grass. I knew he was a marero because of the 13 on his forearm. There was a portrait of the Virgin Mary extending up from the numbers, and I kept my eyes on hers, pleading up; they seemed to know there was little worth seeing in the earthly realm. He was just a teenager, Ana. This fact made it easier to forgive or at least spread blame. The war made a family out of orphaned boys. So did a country that didn't want them either. Deportation. Mara, 18th Street, these were the parents who wanted them. If this makes you think to hate the country that birthed you, to hate yourself, remember that the guns bore US seals. That the last man your grandfather saw before a bullet to the face had just returned from a Georgia training camp.

The man who made you, and undid me, came as a warning. Your uncle, my brother, had a little store and he paid dues. But then there were some rough months. There was no money. He'd missed two months of payment. When they came the third month, they beat him up. I was the only warning left.

You are not of the man who raped me. I decided this as soon as I knew I was pregnant. I don't believe a person is a person until they've arrived, announced themselves as such. I believe family is whoever we point to. I did not just have you. You did not simply happen to me. I chose. I saw the possibilities and I chose and I would not judge the woman who chooses differently. I decided I would be your mother and family, and you would be of me. I tell you this story but I do not call him your father.

Did I tell you about the day you were born? You were a month early, not too early for the doctors to consider you premature but early enough that you looked frail and tiny, smaller than all the other babies in the hospital. To me, you were a speck, a feather, and I was afraid you would die. It's a horrible thought, I know. But probably the first thought in every mother's mind: *So many ways I could fail at this.* I was afraid to hold you, even. I was alone in the hospital and the nurse must have thought me tragic because she prayed a rosary over me. Out of politeness I didn't ask her to stop. But I remember I thought, for the first time, *My God. Nobody asked you either, Mary. Nobody asked if God could build a temple out of you, if you wanted to turn your life into an offering.*

They killed your uncle six months later, you still latched to my chest, you still sleeping in a bundle by my side. I will spare you the details and say only this: I made a choice again, for you. And I am sorry I had nothing else to offer, Ana. That there are no real rules that govern why some are born in turmoil and others never know a single day in which the next seems an ill-considered bet. It's all lottery, Ana, all chance. It's the flick of a coin, and we are born.

6

PREY

Carmen
Miami, 2016

Carmen was setting a bird-of-paradise centerpiece among the linen place mats when she heard the guttural growl, a persistent rumble that sharpened into an alarm. It sounded almost like Linda—her blue Siamese—when a bird in flight mocked the cat's predatory wiggles from the safer side of the sliding glass door. But this shriek went far beyond a pitch Linda could emit. This shriek had the unmistakable texture of wildness.

Not that Carmen would have known. In Coral Gables, the wildest residents were peacocks, lazy pageant queens traversing between parked Aston Martins on hedge-hidden driveways. Carmen had been to a zoo exactly once, some twenty years ago, as a chaperone for one of Jeanette's elementary school classes. As far as she could remember, none of the lions had growled. Neither had the cheetahs or the white tigers. She'd found, on a whole, the zoo an entirely forgettable experience. But she must have seen a nature show at least once in her sixty-odd years (who could even remember their own age anymore?) because somewhere in her mind's gathered archives an immediate connection formed: the noise came from a wild beast, a beast that didn't belong in the civilized world.

She'd told guests to arrive at 7 p.m. It was three o'clock. The turkey glowed beneath the oven's lights, crisping. She'd set all fifteen places. Carmen had chosen a hybrid décor, the usual Thanksgiving stand-ins with some tropical flourishes: a cornucopia filled with cascading autumn vegetables nestled among marble figurines on a hallway table, single lipstick-red hibiscus blooms in crystal vases throughout the living room.

Still clutching a few stray petals that had drifted from the centerpiece, she left the house in yoga pants and house slippers to investigate. Carmen looked up and down the street and the scene was as always—the street empty and quiet and grandiose, the banyan trees arched in a canopy like kissing lovers, her neighbors tucked safely in their own houses or out already for early dinners. Ever since her husband's death— she felt ill even thinking of him, the pervert—she'd thought Coral Gables the loveliest and loneliest neighborhood in the whole world. Its faux-Spanish street markers, its vine-laden fences and stone gateways: all flourish, all enamel, hiding nothing, just persistent *nothing* beneath.

She was about to turn back when she heard it again, another growl. It came, definitively, from the house across the street. How strange, she thought. Perhaps the single woman who lived in the house watched a loud movie. But not likely. She couldn't shake the weirdness as she showered, as she dressed in her dark blue Ralph Lauren suit (a suit she hadn't worn since retirement). And after she'd placed seltzer in an ice bucket to chill, after she'd laid out chips and cornichons beside her homemade paté, she crossed the street.

She had meant only to knock. But Carmen startled at drops of what looked like blood, a trail from the center of the driveway to the door, a sprinkling of dark crimson she'd missed from the safety of her own driveway. She was so taken aback she crouched to the ground and looked closer, as if blood could speak its truth if only she leaned into it. But she gathered herself and stood, forced her wild thoughts to heel. This wasn't a movie. She wasn't a heroic amateur detective, much as she loved those shows.

Every window was curtained, and there were no cars in the driveway. She braced herself and knocked but nobody opened the door. She knew little about the occupant other than she was a single woman like herself, a woman with a grown child just like her, though this child was far more functional than Jeanette: a man who sometimes stopped by with kids and a wife in tow. The woman was like Carmen but far less put-together. And she talked too much. The woman let her gray roots sprawl, she wore pilled knit shirts and was often clacking about her garden in plastic flip-flops, waving to Carmen with garden shears in her hand, swiping her forehead with a rag. She'd talk about her son, about how her daughter-in-law was lazy and clearly taking advantage of him, about how *menopause was killing her* for God's sake. It was like the woman had no filter, no sense that some thoughts belonged in the hidden parts of herself.

Carmen was about to turn back when she thought she heard footsteps. But no lights came on. The door remained shut. She put her ear to the wood and heard the slow hum of an empty house and then, almost imperceptibly, a long sigh, like a dog curling into sleep. No, not a dog. The footsteps rang heavy, the breathing not a pant but an audible purring. Like Linda's purrs but through a stethoscope, magnified, huge. For a moment, she had the irrational idea that a house might have a living, breathing soul, a heart trapped among shine-polished appliances and old inherited furniture, bursting to be known. Perhaps bleeding into the street. She stumbled back from the door. Then crept forward again, put her ear to it again. Yes, purring.

A part of her liked the idea of a monster waiting to burst into Coral Gables, waiting to devour Carmen's cousins and old aunts, their adult children, her fifteen guests. She couldn't shake her fear at the strange confluence of blood and loud breathing, but she was too nervous about Thanksgiving dinner to give her imaginative leaps much real estate, to spend time or energy on anything but dinner. She forced herself to think of harmless explanations—*Who hasn't cut themselves on some sharp object or another and unknowingly left a trail of blood? Who is to say a cat can't sound like a lion under the right conditions?* Jeanette was fresh out of treatment, only two months living out of the facility. It had been her third stay. Carmen wanted everything perfect, though she had little hope for Jeanette's continuing sobriety.

At home, Carmen chilled a second bottle of seltzer. She set out more chips, two appetizer stations at opposite sides of the living room. In an hour, her first guests would arrive. She had decided to invite Jeanette for their first Thanksgiving together in years, so many years.

Before this, she had banned Jeanette. Carmen had told her point-blank: she would no longer support her, she would no longer invite her to any family functions, she would no longer be her mother until Jeanette could prove that she was really, truly sober. Such a decision would likely have seemed, to any mother on the outside, cruel. But no mother on the outside could possibly know what it was to face a truth like the one she'd been presented with: that it was her own love killing her daughter, that she needed to become stone, marble, not a mother at all, to save her daughter. Now Carmen would see her daughter for the first time since driving her to detox and then rehab, again.

Jeanette arrived last, long after the steady stream of relatives, one after the other, carrying aluminum trays covered in foil and bottles of fruit juice, as if no one knew what to bring in place of wine. She had told her guests not to bring alcohol but she hadn't said why. She hadn't said *recovery* or *drugs* or even *my daughter*. She knew they knew why. That was her family, unwilling to name the truth as it danced like dander in the periphery.

Jeanette greeted Carmen as if the two had just seen each other: airy kiss on the cheek and airy chitchat—how hot *is it* out there?—between handfuls of chips. The noise in the house had grown to a level that would drown out any wild growls.

"By the way, Mom," Jeanette said, smoothing an errant curl behind her ear and leaving a trail of crumbs beneath her, "Mario is coming but he couldn't get ready in time. I gave him the address."

"Are you kidding me?" Each syllable strained against the others unnaturally.

Jeanette waved a hand in front of her face as if to say *It's nothing, don't worry.* "He's sober now too, Mom. It's completely different. And we're not, like, *together.* He's being a really good friend."

Jeanette looked away. Her eyes darted, seemed to take in the whole room, all the clusters of conversation.

"Anyways, it's not like *you* can judge."

That familiar sharp, stabbing pain. Carmen wanted to say something back. But she couldn't.

Jeanette looked sober, though, Carmen thought. Her curls were neatly moussed and bouncy; she wore fresh, precise makeup. Carmen would've preferred she wear something a little more *celebratory* than jeans and a tight-fitting tank top but she couldn't deny that, in her late twenties, Jeanette could pull off looking good in almost anything. Still, she seemed distracted, jumping from conversation to conversation, ducking each time talk turned toward her. Carmen stood on the margin, gripping a glass of fruit juice, afraid to approach her daughter as if she'd catch a whiff of some hidden sorrow if she got too close. Could this be all there was to it—Jeanette would get sober? Mario too? Life would continue as if the past five years had happened to someone else?

And there was the other fact keeping Carmen hyper-perceptive—she couldn't shake the noise, the guttural growl; she couldn't shake the blood. She found herself losing the thread of conversations and turning toward her living room window, her guests trailing off. And then she'd turn back to that person, an aunt or a cousin or their spouse: *You were saying?*

But then Rosalinda's husband, Pepe, had pulled a flask out of his back pocket and poured its contents into a water glass. Carmen saw him do it. She had set the table without wine stems or highballs. She'd set the table with only water glasses. Carmen sidled up to Pepe, made a show of staring at the glass in his hand.

"You're looking younger, Carmen," he said. Pepe leaned a hand on her mahogany side table. "You're looking more like Jeanette." He took a sip. "Me, I just get older. I was never one to coddle my Vanessa, you know. That's probably what keeps you young. When you don't coddle them, it's stressful. But it's better not to coddle, it's definitely better."

Pepe's slender wiry daughter appeared as if on cue, whisking the glass out of his hand and taking a sip herself. "I heard that," she said.

"Now, Papi." Vanessa smiled at Carmen. She'd left a dark-red lipstick ring on the glass. "Everyone knows you're the world's biggest coddler. Tía, come." She took Carmen by the arm as if leading a child.

In the kitchen, Vanessa poured Pepe's liquor into the sink, and it looked like dark brown blood circling into the drain. Vanessa started to ask after Jeanette but Carmen squeezed past her. She needed to keep tabs on her daughter.

But her daughter sat absorbed in conversation with her great-aunt Mercedes and Vanessa's brother Tomás, who struggled to hold a hissing Linda in his arms as the cat's eyes darted from face to face in fear.

"She clearly doesn't like being held," Aunt Mercy said to Tomás. Linda began to claw frantically.

"Fuck!" Tomás yelled. He let the cat go, and she darted into the hallway.

"Oh." Jeanette placed her plate of hummus on a chair and examined the scratches blooming on Tomás's arms. "Let me get you a bandage."

"No!" Carmen yelled over the din. "I'll get it!"

———

In the bathroom, Carmen closed her eyes. She visualized the cheerful, welcoming hostess she wanted her family to see. *Martha Stewart,* she told herself. *Nitza Villapol.* She opened her eyes. Carmen shuffled out with a bottle of rubbing alcohol in one hand and loose bandages in the other.

Mario stood in the middle of the living room with a bouquet of grocery-store carnations. He wore black pants and a thermal much too warm for Miami in November. Jeanette grabbed Mario's hand and pulled him toward Carmen.

"Hasn't it been *forever* since you saw Mario?" she called, her tone artificially cheerful, too nervous and fidgety.

Mario didn't meet Carmen's eyes, but he gave her a tepid hug. Carmen wanted to scream at him, blame him for something, anything, for everything, but she tried to remain composed, tried to remain *Martha Stewart*.

She looked after every detail. Appetizers restocked, toilet paper in the bathrooms, AC temperature right. She looked after every detail to avoid thinking about blood, to avoid looking at Jeanette, to avoid mixing the two.

———

The conversation, once everyone sat for dinner, was painstaking, fifteen people desperately waiting their turn to insert an opinion, nobody concerned with what anybody else thought about anything. Perhaps every conversation played out like this, and it was only now, aware of every move, every reaction, that Carmen realized it was a miracle human beings learned anything about each other at all.

"So what do you do, Mario?"

"Is there pork too? I always say it's not a real feast without some puerco asado."

"I'm in retail."

"In Cuba, every party, there was pork. Every party, a pig killed."

"That's right! No pork, no party."

"Retail?"

Jeanette barely spoke. As usual, she shriveled in Mario's presence. Jeanette moved the food around her plate and looked from person to person and occasionally sighed and dabbed her lips with a corner of napkin. Carmen smiled politely when her second cousin Vivian's husband complimented her truffled mashed potatoes. She laughed when her uncle, eighty-nine and still a chain smoker, told an unfunny political joke. She asked a question or two about her other second cousin Delia's new job in real estate. But then Pepe got out of hand again.

"How is Dolores?" he said, turning to Carmen. He knew, like their entire family knew, that Carmen didn't speak to her mother.

"You know, I spoke to Maydelis in Cuba, Jeanette," he said, not even waiting for an answer. "She said Dolores won't stop asking about you. She tells Maydelis constantly that you and her must work to reunite the family."

"I love Maydelis," Jeanette said. "We email all the time. I'd love to go to Cuba. Maydelis says—"

"Listen," Carmen interrupted. "Dolores just means to make trouble—"

"You mean your mother—"

"I mean Dolores—"

"Hey, you know what I learned, Jeanette?" Pepe's daughter said, staring him down and turning to Jeanette. "Our great-grandmother Cecilia worked at a tobacco factory that still makes cigars." Jeanette looked uneasy, balling the napkin in her hand. "And our great-great-grandparents probably, our great-great-great-grandparents probably. Like, this whole legacy and you can just buy one of these cigars and like you feel like you're holding all this history in your hand but you don't really know what it means and—"

Mario stood, clearly sensing the tension, and said something like "Speaking of cigars, I need a cigarette break."

Vanessa, always with her froufrou talk, always talking too much. Jeanette asked Mario if he wanted her to go with him. He told her to stay. Carmen excused herself a beat later.

Outside the street was empty, peaceful, her family's cars packed in the driveway and spilling onto the curb, announcing that hers was a full home. She could hear the stream of conversation as she closed the door. Cuba this, Cuba that.

Cuba Cuba Cuba. Why anyone left a place only to reminisce, to carry its streets into every conversation, to see every moment through the eyes of some imagined loss, was beyond her. Miami existed as such a hollow receptacle of memory, a shadow city, full of people who needed a place to put their past into perspective. Not her. She lived in the present.

Carmen was surprised to find that Mario had crossed the street, that he stood on the lawn of the neighbor's house, the monster house. He faced away from her, so he couldn't know that she was there, watching him. Mario shook a cigarette pack on the palm of his hand and pulled one out. He lit it with a hand cupped around the flame. Then he took something else out of his pocket, something orange, a small cylinder.

As if on cue, Carmen heard the growl from before, the shriek, as Mario flinched and dropped his cigarette.

"What was that?" she yelled, rushing to his side. "What was that?"

Mario turned to face her, his mouth agape. "I—don't know," he said. "It sounded like . . . a lion almost?"

"No!" Carmen yelled. "In your hand! What was that? A medicine bottle, wasn't it? You're trying to ruin her again, aren't you?"

Mario's mouth still hung open, and he looked at Carmen as if taking her in for the first time. She regretted the suit, felt ridiculous in her sensible heels, sweat rolling down her back. She wondered what Jeanette had told Mario. If she shared too much, if she talked too much. But Carmen felt triumphant. She felt like she was confronting someone for the first time in her life. A hunter. He was the lion seeping blood into the street. He was the lion dirtying her beautiful neighborhood.

Mario dug into his pocket again and pulled out a prescription bottle.

"I knew it!" Carmen screamed.

Mario handed the bottle to her and Carmen looked at the label. Prilosec. Her late husband had taken the same prescription antacid. He had suffered from terrible heartburn. When they walked back to the house, Mario didn't mention the growl again. They didn't speak at all.

———·———

Inside, Carmen began to clear plates loudly though Rosalinda still picked at the congrí. Her guests quieted in her presence. Diana's eight-year-old daughter—or was she Susana's daughter? there were too many children to keep track of—followed her into the kitchen. Carmen could hear laughter in the dining room.

"Hi," the someone's daughter said. "My mom said guests should bring their plates to the kitchen."

"Oh," Carmen said, annoyed. She didn't want to speak to anyone. "That is very nice of you, Ana."

"That's not my name," the girl whose name wasn't Ana said.

Carmen snapped off her rubber gloves. She leaned against the counter and considered the child.

"My name is Lila," Lila said.

Ana, Ana. It came to her, why she'd called her that.

Lila squinted up at her.

Nowadays, it was all over the Spanish-language news: the ICE raids, the young people in graduation caps handcuffed to congressional desks, saying this is my home, let me stay. Red-faced men on TV shows snarling *alien,* snarling *jobs,* snarling *it's about time we take back our country.* Our country. Take back. She didn't agree with some of the other Cubans her age who said things like *we're* not like them, *we* belong here, *we're* political refugees. Carmen had lost a parent, her father. And she knew that rip, that tear, that hollow feeling like a tooth pulled, forever something *off, forever a space*. Jeanette thought her so old-fashioned, so backward in her opinions. But no, she was fair. She wanted families together. Shouldn't that count for something?

"I'm going to Cuba in three weeks," Lila Not-Ana said.

"Oh, that's nice," Carmen said.

If she could go back in time, maybe she would have helped the girl, Ana, though she had no idea *how*. But *police*. She'd thought *police*. She wondered where that girl could be now. Hopefully, here. Hopefully, home. Some of those same Cubans said, these new Cubans, coming now, they get here and turn right back around and go back to Cuba, and they want the government to give them everything, they are not *like us*. They also said immigrants from other countries weren't like them. Like us. As if she were like anyone. She was more fair-minded, she thought, she didn't even mind the New Cubans, Jeanette didn't understand.

"My mom says you won't go to Cuba. That you won't even talk to your own mother because of *politics*," Not-Ana said. "And she doesn't think it's very nice and she says family is what's most important and she says thank God *we* know how important family is and how we all need to be together and she . . ."

Carmen stared, astounded. Had Jeanette blurted her business this way as a little girl? She couldn't imagine it. Did she do that *now*?

"Well, tell *your* mom—"

"Lila!" Jeanette carried a pile of plates balanced on her forearm into the kitchen as if she were an actual waitress. "Pero how *big* you are."

"You're not big," Lila said with a shrug. She fake-curtsied and walked off, giant bow on her red velvet dress bouncing up and down.

"I don't like her," Carmen said, taking the plates from Jeanette.

"She's literally a *child*, Mom."

"Some children talk too much. You never talked so much."

"Oookay, Mom," Jeanette said. "Anyways, I think me and Mario should go." She held the dishwasher open.

"What? We haven't even had dessert yet. Vivian made pumpkin pie, Mercedes brought a flan."

"I feel like everyone is judging me, you most of all." Jeanette ran a hand over the marble countertop. Carmen tried to decipher a code in her eyes—were they red? Was she just tired? Were everyone's eyes always somewhat red? She wondered if her daughter was the kind of woman who would leave a trail of blood without even noticing.

"Honey, nobody even knows about your . . . problems."

Jeanette leaned back. She let the dishwasher door dangle open. "That's just the thing," she said. "I feel like all you care about is how people see you. How they see me. I feel like I'm constantly pretending, constantly afraid to say the wrong thing."

Carmen wondered if Mario felt strange at the dinner table without Jeanette, whether he talked with other guests or felt like she would, counting the seconds until Jeanette returned. Carmen wondered if Mario would tell Jeanette about their encounter.

"You still don't even tell the truth about Dad," Jeanette said. "Every therapist I've spoken with says that's unhealthy."

Carmen's hands shook as she rinsed each plate and placed it in its slot in the dishwasher. Of course it always came back to this, and each time it felt like an accusation, like Jeanette faulted her for what had happened even if she'd never say that. Carmen placed a rinsed spoon in its receptacle, and she felt the bile rise. To be around Jeanette was too painful. Was that the real reason she'd banned her? Had she just forgotten?

Of course Carmen hadn't known about the abuse. For God's sake, she'd stayed with Julio *because* she'd thought he had a level of love and affection for Jeanette that would dissipate under the weight of separate homes. Because she, Carmen, knew better than anyone what it was to lose a father. She'd never understand why Jeanette had waited until Julio *died* to tell her. Why she had let Carmen mourn this man, live with him all those years, sleep in a bed beside him. This man who was now an infection eating through her. She would have killed him had she known. She would have *called the police*. Would that have saved Jeanette? Even she knew that was a lie.

Jeanette had told her on the day of her husband's funeral. She'd shown up slurring, moving from corner of the room to corner of the room like each one held an opposing magnetic force and she just could not find her place, falling asleep each time she sat down. Other mourners eyed her, cast sidelong glances at one another. And Carmen, furious, had thought, *How could you do this? How could you do this to your* father? She had kicked Jeanette out and continued to greet guests as if nothing had happened. She'd said Jeanette didn't feel well.

But Jeanette had returned. Carmen sat in an armchair, just outside the viewing room that contained Julio's body. She'd tired of guests munching on crackers and standing around as if a dead body were nothing more than a prop, nothing more than a print on the wall or background music or a vase.

"I'm not leaving," Jeanette said.

Carmen stood. She told Jeanette she'd disrespected her father's memory.

"My father's memory?" Jeanette laughed harshly.

"Do you *know* how lucky you are to even have *had* a father?"

At that, Jeanette had grabbed Carmen's arm and stared at her, wild eyed. "That father is the reason for All. Of. This." Jeanette motioned at herself.

"How dare you blame a man who—!"

"A man who—" Her face changed, turned serious. "A man who molested me?"

And Carmen felt the whole room shift, close in on them.

Her words should have been *How?* or *When?* or *I believe you.* Or nothing. Just her body, holding Jeanette's close. Jeanette began to sob.

She remembered the feeling of hovering over the scene. Her daughter shuddering. The guests who walked past assuming Jeanette mourned her father. The flower vendors with the wreaths. That flower smell. Stale. The light bulb. The door. The heat, the heat, even in the overly air-conditioned room.

Her words should have been—any other words. But the real Carmen floated somewhere in the distance. And the body said, "It can't be. It can't be. Are you sure you—?"

But she absolutely knew it *could* be. How many nights had she woken to drunken Julio over her body? How many times had she fought him off and then given in, thinking, *I'm married to him, isn't this just duty?* How the violation had strangled her, how she'd willed herself another life. She had thought herself a bad wife.

Carmen collapsed in the stale-flower-scented bathroom of the Rodríguez Funeral Home. She'd contemplated crawling into a casket herself. When she left the bathroom, Jeanette was gone.

———·———

The dishwasher began its cycle with a lurch of swishing water, the stop-and-start of the jets. Carmen could hear the inappropriate child, Lila, loudly answering questions in the dining room as the adults laughed.

"Maybe we should serve dessert," she said.

Ha ha ha went the whole dining room. Someone smacked the table.

"Mom," Jeanette said. "Asking me a few basic questions about what happened, one time, does not equal meaningful conversation. Do you know what it took for me to tell you?"

Carmen could smell the funeral home again—ugh, the flowers, she hated the flowers. Why? Why dwell, why talk, what good would it do? She had mastered a life without unearthing her own horror stories. She wished Jeanette could do the same. Her daughter needed strength, she needed Carmen's strength for the both of them, she needed to learn the past haunted only if you let it.

"I have to go check on something," she said, already walking out.

She could feel Jeanette watch her, could imagine her exasperated face. Carmen walked out of the kitchen, down the hallway, walked past her guests with their faces turned to her, walked out the door. She could hear the conversation die down to a trickle and then silence as the latch of the front door clicked shut. She imagined Mercy turning to Pepe—*Where did she go?* She imagined Jeanette struggling to serve a flan, imagined her staring at her stacks of serving utensils in confusion.

The pervert, the sick sick man, the poor excuse for a human being, he who should have met a fate worse than liver failure. Her heels clacked loud on the pavement. *My beautiful daughter. My beautiful, beautiful, lost daughter.* Her daughter needed her. No, she wouldn't abandon her this time. She couldn't. She would be a part of Jeanette's life, sober or not, she would, she must.

The other house. Again nobody answered at the other house. Carmen knocked and knocked. She walked across the driveway past the garage and turned. A fence separated the house from the next one, like her own. A small stone path cut to a low gate at the backyard. There was a trash bin and a recycling one. There was a small window perched inches over her head. Carmen stood on tiptoe and peered in. She could scarcely make out a bathroom curtain. She had never understood windows in bathrooms. Why not just a vent of some sort if humidity was the problem? Windows, so many windows. Florida was obsessed with windows.

It was dark now. But the heat hadn't let up. Carmen could feel the moisture bunching on her lower back, into the folds of her suit. She could imagine her carefully sculpted curls frizzing into clown hair. She felt like a clown, creeping around someone else's house, pushing back the words that surfaced despite a refusal to accept them as her thoughts: *It was minor abuse.* He'd touched Jeanette twice only, over her clothes. Just her breasts, Jeanette had said. That *minor* and *abuse* could even fit in the same sentence seemed preposterous. There was no *minor* in abuse, there was no *Thank God, it could have been worse.* Sexual abuse was no car accident. Sexual abuse was no spectrum. Was it?

The backyard gate wasn't locked. Carmen left her kitten heels at the threshold and stepped onto the soft mowed lawn in her stockings. The backyard had a pool and a smaller Jacuzzi lit up from beneath like a deep candle in a tall glass.

There was a ceilinged patio with a built-in bar and huge chrome barbecue. She tiptoed toward the sliding glass doors covered with thick vertical blinds. She put her face to the glass so a circle of her breath fogged and dissipated on the surface. She placed an ear to the cool surface. Again it was like placing a head over a chest and listening to the heartbeat: the hum of the air-conditioning, the barely perceptible groans of an empty house settling into itself. She could hear no cat or tiger or lion. Had she imagined it all? Was she so desperate to think every other home held violence lurking?

A motion-detector light came on and illuminated everything in grotesque shadow. But no alarm had gone off, at least no alarm had gone off. Carmen imagined what she'd look like if the police showed up, barefoot in a sweaty suit pressed up against the glass. She wondered if this was what the Bottom felt like, that undefinable point of addiction when it could get no worse.

She'd read it somewhere once: about someone dying, alone, and the house cat eating pieces of her dead flesh bit by bit. It was supposed to be a cautionary tale, a sad, morbid truth to be faced: *Cats aren't your friend, you pathetic, lonely idiot.* And yet she remembered not feeling that way. She remembered thinking it a practical afterlife, to become useful finally, food not dust.

Carmen hadn't expected the unlocked sliding glass door, really she hadn't. Her hand traveled almost of its own accord and she was shocked to feel the levers give way, the door seamlessly slide to an opening of her size. She'd never done anything like this. The blinds rustled. A burst of cool air hit her face and before she knew it, she was parting the blinds, she was stepping into a stranger's home.

She closed the door behind her. The living room was dark, illuminated by only the fuzzy trickles of fluorescent light from the patio. She could make out marble statuettes, a wrought iron bird cage, multiple glass menageries full of crystal and ceramic figurines. The walls were almost completely covered by painting after painting, a collection grotesquely mismatched—stoic Renaissance portraits, abstract linear sketches, tacky pop art à la Romero Britto. The living room, what she could make of it in the dark, was like a museum basement of cast-offs.

Carmen felt along the wall for a light switch and found one. The awful scene came alive before her in even harsher truth: brocade couch, oversized armchairs draped in velvet and silk tapestry, a swear-to-God actual bearskin rug with taxidermied head intact. Every square inch of the home was swathed in its own expensive and ugly décor. The panorama was so overwhelming that Carmen almost missed it: the huge metal cage nestled into a corner near the front door, reaching almost to the ceiling. Inside lay a curled, sleeping figure beside a water bowl and a slab of untouched still-bloody meat, beside a trail of blood drops leading to the front door.

Carmen's hand went to her mouth in almost choreographed, cinematic precision. She crept toward the metal enclosure, nerves rattled, her whole body trembling in excitement and terror.

As if sensing her nearing presence, the creature stirred and sat up. Its lips curled and a long hiss escaped between needle-sharp incisors. A panther, a young one. She identified the panther almost immediately without knowing she held *Florida panther* in her mind's encyclopedia of feline species. Carmen leaned closer, ignored the animal's cautionary sounds. As if challenged, the panther's hissing got louder. And then they just stared at each other.

Carmen marveled at the similarities between the panther and her cat Linda: the ears, parallel and curved back, the tight wiring of the whiskers, the way the nose slightly quivered. But there were differences too: the sinewy muscles that rippled the panther's sleek skin as if readying to pounce, the way its long teeth glistened like ivory knives. Some part of her, almost against her will but perhaps not really, wanted to reach over and open the cage, wanted to smear herself in blood and feel the body give way in sacrifice. To be an animal, to carry nothing of the past, nothing past the immediate need to satiate a hunger. She wouldn't take it personally if the panther attacked. She would understand. She would forgive. She was so caught up in the moment she almost missed the headlights that moved a spotlight over the cage, almost didn't hear the crunchy, gravelly sound of a car coming to a stop in front of the house.

Carmen remembered herself. Remembered Jeanette, remembered her guests. She ran, the animal growling as she slammed shut the sliding glass door just as a key turned the lock of the front one, ran past the pool and around the corner, grabbing her shoes with one swift motion, crouching at the edge of the house, peering to her right, heart thumping thumping thumping, making sure the car's inhabitants were inside, nobody there waiting to find her. She could not believe herself. Carmen as a cartoon, a *Looney Tune,* predator circling one side, she the outsmarting prey. Duck season, rabbit season. She nearly laughed. She nearly laughed as she ran in her stockings across the street. They would never know. They would never know.

Of course, she'd gather herself before she walked back into her own home. Bending to see herself in the side mirror of her car, she'd smooth her hair as best she could. She'd take off the jacket with the sweat stains blooming and stay in her silk sleeveless blouse, even though she hated her flabby upper arms and thought it imprudent for a woman over fifty to bare legs past the knee or arms above the elbow. She'd consider calling the cops once again, she'd even quickly search *Miami animal control* and *report exotic animals* on her phone, before deciding to keep the secret. She'd keep the secret as she walked into her own home with an excuse about needing to move her car as Jeanette eyed her strangely. She'd keep the secret each time she waved to her frumpy neighbor from her own threshold. She'd keep the secret when she drove Jeanette to detox again, Mario sweaty and red beside her. She'd keep the secret even when, five years later, the panther would escape its cage and maul its owner, the woman who spoke too much, leading to five skin grafts and a face Carmen would never look at again and a newspaper article in which neighbors expressed shock—they'd had no idea!—and the woman would be quoted: "It could have been worse. I'm just grateful to be alive, my God, it could have been worse."

7

PRIVILEGIO

Ana, Irapuato, 2018

Mexico morphed her language. A *chele* became a *güero,* a *guineo* transformed into a *plátano*. Her Spanish grew stronger than her English again but her accent began to change. Trying to Mexicanize a stubborn tongue to fit in. Hearing the derogatory comments. Gente de afuera taking over the city, bringing crime, taking jobs, pinches cerotes, call the Migra, send them home. Some Mexicans kind, welcoming. Not all. Easier to try to blend in, easier to try on a new camouflage (also painful). Also confusing. Her mother promised every year they'd go back, they just needed to save a little more money. A lot more money. Maybe they'd never go back?

It'd been four years already. Ana and her mother were still in Mexico. She'd known almost as much life in Miami as in Irapuato.

Here, she worked. For a US-born woman with flowing red hair. Doña Nancy. Well, technically she didn't *work* for Nancy. Gloria, her mother, did. But Ana had always helped her mother, for years she had helped her mother, and Nancy finally offered Ana pay. The previous muchacha had started working in a kitchen when she was eight years old after her father died. As a girl she'd been able to buy shoes for all her sisters, and this had been a source of great pride. Ana heard her tell Gloria this story before the woman left her post to marry.

"I want to work too," Ana had said to Doña Nancy some years back. Nancy had said no but agreed to give Ana an allowance for helping her mother. Plus Ana wasn't going to school; Gloria taught her with books Nancy brought home from the middle school where she taught English. So Ana was working, but she wasn't. It was all very confusing. She spent all her time around adults.

———·———

Nancy liked everything really, really hot. She liked a quesadilla that could set off a smoke alarm when you unfolded the tortilla. She liked her soup still bubbling in the bowl. If you served Nancy food, and it wasn't scorching hot, Nancy would frown and then she'd get up and microwave her plate. So Ana charred everything, skirted burning every meal. She often scorched her fingers taking plates to the dinner table.

You learned these kinds of things about people, their habits, their eccentricities, when you worked for them. Ana knew Nancy better than Nancy's own husband, who sometimes sought Ana's advice over a birthday gift or anniversary plan, which her mother thought was an outrageous thing to ask a child. Sometimes he'd even ask Ana about Nancy's schedule.

For instance, Roberto probably didn't notice that Nancy never wiped her feet on the bath mat when she got out of the shower, instead leaving a trail of watery footprints that required listening for the turn of the faucet, the opening of the bathroom door, so Ana could be ready with the mop.

Roberto probably didn't know that Nancy smoked cigarettes sometimes while he was at work and then hid the carton in the upper-right drawer of their shared wardrobe between the neat rows of panties Ana folded each week.

Or that Ana had caught Nancy kissing her Spanish teacher in her driveway one morning while Roberto was at work and that no one said anything and Nancy had given her mother a raise two days later.

That Nancy liked to fidget by stretching a hair tie with her fingers, or picking at a piece of thread, or scratching off her nail polish.

That Nancy had a hidden stack of cash beneath a floorboard.

———·———

Doña Nancy spoke terrible Spanish but she managed to survive in a city like Irapuato where few tourists had reason to visit and not many people spoke English. She'd arrived, after several years of floundering from job to job in the States, to teach English at one of the private middle schools. She'd met Roberto by chance, on a weekend visit to Guanajuato. Roberto was taking a New York client on a tour of the mummy museum and in between an exhibit of a mummified fetus and one that wore socks, Nancy struck a conversation, delighted to meet an English-speaking Mexican whom she could pepper with questions. They exchanged numbers and two years later had a house in one of the new luxury colonias popping up all over Irapuato and a dual citizenship that allowed her to live in Mexico indefinitely.

Ana knew all this because Nancy loved to chat her up at the dining table as her mother swept and mopped circles around them. Ana liked that Nancy spoke to her as if she were any of the other adults in her life and not a twelve-year-old girl. Nancy said she had stood up for Ana and her mother, had vocally argued to keep them in the home even though Roberto had not wanted a Salvadoreña maid. It was typical, this attitude, Nancy said to Ana when telling her about how she'd fought for their hiring, as if Ana weren't acutely aware of the bias she herself faced.

"He means well," Nancy said to her that day, "but how do you undo what is so ingrained? I mean, Roberto has so much *privilege*. Privilegio. Do you know what that word means?"

Nancy liked to sprinkle her speech with Spanish even though Ana spoke English. Ana nodded though she wasn't sure.

———

The first day they'd been in the home, Gloria had served their food in a separate part of the house, a little room off the kitchen, where the two of them could eat out of sight. But Nancy had swept in and said no, no, they were now part of the family, *of course* they *had* to eat with her and Roberto, and they had all eaten together in mostly silence as Roberto glared and Nancy directed questions that her mother answered with a quiet humility Ana had never seen in her, and she wished they could just eat, alone, in the little room so she could just stop . . . *performing*. But that was years ago. Now she liked being around Nancy. She wanted so badly to *be* Nancy. Not of here but with a *not-of-hereness* that evoked curiosity and interest, maybe humor, like when Nancy went to the mercado and her Spanish was met with amusement, with kindness. Nancy in a huipil, her hair in ribboned braids. Nancy telling the Indigenous artesanos at the market how beautiful they wove. Nancy with the *not-of-hereness* people smiled at, just a little bit of smirk. Said *here, come, take*.

———

Her mother wasn't the doting type. Ana had made her a card once, for Mother's Day, and written *Thank you for sacrific-*

ing everything for me. "Is that what you think?" Gloria asked her that night. "That I'm supposed to sacrifice everything for you?" Ana hadn't understood what she did wrong, what she could have possibly said that was wrong. Her mother apologized shortly after, thanked her for the card, told her that she loved her, that she was tired. She knew her mother was tired. That's why she helped. That's why she *worked*.

That's why she walked the blocks around Doña Nancy's colonia watching the rich kids kick balls around the skeletons of new construction feeling so much older, too old for shrieking, too old for candy-sticky skin, too old for looking so free. Until a boy said hi one day, asked her age, until she replied with her new accent and, yes, of course, they were the same age.

Go play, her mother would say in the early days. Go play, Doña Nancy would say, showing up from the mercado with a wooden ball on a string attached to a bucket. A doll. A Jacob's ladder.

Doña Nancy taking her to Cristalita to eat frozen strawberries with cream, sugared strawberries, everything strawberry in the city of strawberries, then buying her a doll. I've never seen anyone treat their maid like she's their child, her mother muttered when Ana got back home with her gifts. I'm not her *maid*, she protested. Her mother smiled.

When she first got to Mexico, baby deportee, the strawberries had made Ana sick. Or maybe it'd been something else. She was sick all the time at first. Doña Nancy said to her: me too.

———·———

They were lost or abandoned or there had been some mix-up. Or this was on purpose. A kindness? A cruelty? A trick? They'd been dropped off over the border in Mexico instead of flown to El Salvador and no one kept track of them. Everyone assumed they were traveling north. Straight off the train tracks and biding time in a city along the path. They just lay low and ducked migra like the rest, knowing they'd make their way back. The first thing her mother had done was call a cousin who lived in Irapuato. The cousin found Gloria this job. She made hardly any money, nothing even close to what she'd earned in Miami, but they had a room. Her mother told her she'd save so Ana wouldn't have to hop trains or walk miles, if she could help it. Burn money on a van, on the most expensive guide. Months whipping by. Years. Doña Nancy: "Who'd want to leave such a beautiful country?" As if anything were about beauty. Or want.

———·———

Her mother wasn't the doting type but Ana knew her mother loved her. Because, look—she, too, cried sometimes talking about the kids playing, about all the other possible lives if *x* or *y* had happened instead of *z*. Saying, I'm so proud of you, all the ways you help me. Gloria loved to dance but she didn't go to dance clubs as she had in Miami anymore. And whenever Ana spied Nancy in the bathroom, carefully applying eyeliner for a night out with Roberto or her "ex-pat" friends, Nancy jiggling her hips to a radio song with a shot of tequila in her hand, she wanted her mother to be Nancy too. She wanted to grow up even faster so maybe she could set her mother free.

———·———

Her last year in Mexico, Gloria got sick. Fast, like one day blood in a tissue and the next there they were, the two of them, huddled in a dark IMSS hospital. (Nancy had paid a doctor to see her even though she had no papers but let them know she couldn't pay long-term.) Doctor saying, Why'd you wait so long? Saying, I don't know, there's not much we can do, would the patrona pay for chemo? I don't know, it's so advanced.

Walking her mother down a hallway, holding her oxygen tank. Helping her onto a bus because Nancy was working and couldn't pick them up. How her mother placed a hand in her lap. Whispered thank you, and Ana wasn't even sure for what.

She remembered curling next to her mother on their twin bed, ear to her chest. To hear her heart. Each labored breath. To will each one. Please please *please*.

———•———

Money in the floorboard. Would chemo buy her more time? She could have taken it but she didn't. She could have taken it because years later Nancy caught Roberto with his mistress, and she raged, she threw her ring down the sink, she left Mexico overnight, she said she was never coming back to that godforsaken place, it'd been her worst mistake, she left without the money, she didn't even remember the money, she was so angry. But how could Ana know? Ana would never know. All she thought at the time was, If she took the money, and if Doña Nancy found out, then where would they go?

8

THEY LIKE THE GRIMY

Maydelis
La Habana, 2015

It isn't cheating if the marriage is on life support. The only reason we haven't pulled the plug is inconvenience: scarce housing. (How many couples who hate each other still live under the same roof here, eating silent meals with the TV turned up to fill the space?)

That's what I tell myself as the man who is not my husband, El Alemán, helps me into the passenger seat, hands me my overnight bag. Jeanette eyes us from the back seat with a knowing smile. "Are you going to tell me what happened?" she whispers as El Alemán walks around to the driver's side door.

I flash a smile I hope says: *Nothing. Everything.*

El Alemán squeezes in and pulls the lever at his side. "Goddamn Russian goddamn piece-of-shit cars!" he yells in English as the seat springs back and Jeanette pulls her knees in. "Who's supposed to fit in this thing?"

"Huh, there's a cup holder," Jeanette says pulling down the center partition that does, indeed, hide a cup holder.

"I thought all you guys were supposed to drive those neat

1950s Chevrolets," El Alemán says. "Why didn't they give me one of those?"

Jeanette sighs.

"I would have brought my cafecito if I knew there was a cup holder." She rests an elbow on the center partition.

"Of course there's a cup holder. What do you think this is? Mars? We're not that backward."

Picture it: me and two foreigners. The patience required. Though I'm more amenable to dishing it out for my cousin than for this sunburned, blustering German on holiday. Outside, the valet porters watch us silently. They're trying to guess the situation, this I know. Two Cuban prostitutes, one tourist? Two tourist relatives and one lucky Cuban family member? A married couple and their hustling tour guide? Porters, *I'm* trying to figure out the situation.

It's that sticky, suffocating kind of summer that makes a shower futile. Already I can taste the sweat, the brine in the air. El Alemán circles the driveway of the Hotel Nacional, Jeanette's hotel—where I stayed last night—and turns where I direct. Then the Malecón zips by: ocean, limestone wall, no waves to temper the heat though that's not deterring children in their underpants from dangling legs in optimistic anticipation. And two fishermen atop the wall, handmade poles in hand. We are nothing if not a hopeful people.

"Even after being here for a week, it still gets me. Everything crumbling. Everything in ruins." Jeanette points to a disintegrating apartment, a woman in a head wrap staring blankly in the doorway.

"But a certain romance, no?" El Alemán casts a look at me. "The crumbling. Everything pastel. The ocean, ah, the ocean."

Any other circumstance and I'd roll my eyes at both of them. But I've learned a special kind of patience, a kind of mask, because tourists are easily hurt. I've learned it from selling knickknacks to foreigners along the Malecón. Work my husband belittles. Hustle my husband doesn't see as work. But I make more money than he does, and he is a doctor. That's why he ridicules me.

What you do is you notice the little details. Like you can tell just from the clothes, you know?

I watch the people on the Malecón as we zoom past. A woman with a small gold cross and three gold rings. Cuban-American, no doubt about it. Back from La Yuma full of gold and jewels trying to impress some folks. They like to hear how hard it is. How it's gotten worse. Yeah, more apagones, the lights just went out yesterday, you missed it. Have you seen what they're giving out in the ration bodegas? Real political. Everything political. If they're real Americanized, I sell them nostalgia, postcards of an old La Habana that existed only in their dreams. I sell them misery in the hopes they give me an extra dollar or two. I gave Jeanette a print of the old Tropicana club in all its glory. "For your mom," I said.

We pass a young gringo, long hair pulled into a bun. Flip-flops, a seashell necklace, tank top. European. Or La Yuma. Doesn't matter. That type: he wants to hear about the *romance,* about how *inspiring* it is to live here. But here, I have to be a little careful. I have to feel it out. Some just want to hear some Buena Vista Social Club, want to hear about how my grandma met Fidel Castro when he rolled through the city in a victory parade. But some of them, they're real political the other way. They ask me all these complicated questions, they want to know what's the *real* deal in Cuba, like there's a secret truth. Education (is it *really* free?), medicine (is it *really* free?). And they want to hear about santería, so I pretend to practice. They want to hear about how we turn peeling apartments with sinking roofs into salsa dance clubs. I tell them I can take them someplace no tourists ever go. I have to remember, they *like* the grimy stuff. They don't want the nice and clean. It's weird. They buy the Che Guevara prints, the vintage revolution pins. Or they just give me money because they assume I need it—even better. They call me *friend*.

We turn on Quinta Avenida and line up for the highway. A dozen people stand by the side of the road, waiting on a truck to pick them up. Jeanette sighs dramatically.

And I'm thinking: a jinetera is not a prostitute. Another thing foreigners don't understand. They think the words are interchangeable. Prostitution would be easy. Prostitution would be in-and-out, collect the cash, efficient transaction.

El Alemán rumbles into traffic, passes a mule hauling a cart, a guajiro. "On the fucking highway," he says. "The *highway*."

A jinetera studies, calculates. And, yes, offers sex sometimes, oftentimes. But so much more to give and parse and offer. And not just a listening ear or a compliment, these, too, the territory of prostitutes. One might, for instance, end up in a car with a US cousin and a German tourist because he wants to take us to a resort on Varadero Beach. One might put up with platitudes feigned as insight.

A lane switch and the landscape gets more rural. More sugarcane, less rubble. Billboards: THE REVOLUTION STARTS WITH YOU. ALWAYS WITH YOU, COMANDANTE. More palm, more sky, more valley. More bodies in truck beds, hair whipping in the wind.

"Ah, this is life," says El Alemán.

"The poverty. The poverty is heartbreaking," says Jeanette.

I just sink back. Time trickles. A countryside lullaby, highway rumble rocking. I close my eyes and picture what it would take to seduce a German tourist into falling in love with me, what it would take to convince a German tourist he needs to marry me, because he needs me, because in his mind I am everything a German woman isn't. I am vacation, my body is vacation. What would it take to convince a German tourist to whisk me away? It happens often enough— Dianelys, Yudi, Leti, all of them somewhere in Europe. I picture how I would get from Germany to Spain, where work would be easier. Would I need to stay married for more than a year?

Then I am awake—a side-of-the-road pork shack, El Alemán nudging me and whispering, "Need you to translate, darling."

We step out of the car to an onslaught of mosquitoes and calf-high saw grass, a shirtless guajiro stirring a vat in the shade of a palm hut. An hour nap? Two hours? I order three pan con pernil and the guajiro smears dripping pulled pork with mojo, a corn husk for a brush. El Alemán takes big bites, leaning on the car and bending forward as grease dribbles down his chin. Jeanette is dainty despite the oil shining her lips, the gnats circling.

What would it take to make a cousin send for me? What would it take to convince her she needs to support me until I can get on my feet in a place like Miami, where there are so many stories like mine? Maybe I could just travel back and forth. Which would require giving more of myself away?

"I need to pee," Jeanette says halfway into her sandwich. She hands me her plate and opens the trunk, digs through her luggage. Toilet paper from the hotel room in hand, she elbows me and tells me to go with her.

We leave our paper plates in the care of El Alemán and trek into the grass, the guajiro watching us from the shack and swatting flies with slimy hands.

"How far we gonna go?" I ask.

"Shhh. I don't even really have to pee."

"What?" Jeanette grabs my wrist and pulls me closer to her. The grass has morphed into cane now. Gnats buzz in my ears when I wipe the slickness from my face. We both crouch in the shadow of the stalks like hiding prey.

"I just couldn't wait," Jeanette says. "Tell me what happened. I'm dying to know."

What is there to say? To this cousin of mine whom I'd never met in person before? She is beautiful—fat black curls and deep-set, almond eyes. She has a strange, lopsided smile. I try to detect signs of what my aunt said when she sent the email announcing Jeanette's trip—of the drug addiction that held her captive for years, of the drama of a failed relationship that tends to age a person. I can detect no signposts of hardship, only a brightness of the eyes, a conspiring touch on the arm that says, *We never knew each other but blood is blood and we can be honest now.*

So I'm as honest as I can be with someone whose life feels so far from my own. I tell her what happened last night after she left me on the long elevated patio of the Hotel Nacional and went to bed. We'd ordered mojito after mojito (even though technically Jeanette wasn't supposed to drink), and tipsy, I'd glanced at the Malecón below, at the couples making out under salty mist, the peanut vendors with their paper cones and singsong advertising. And I'd considered the events of the night: the unattractive German man who'd chatted us up, who'd asked so nonchalantly if we'd like to join him on a trip to Varadero. Jeanette had said no. I'd said yes. Courage

up from the rum warming my throat I'd pulled her into furtive whispers in the bathroom of the hotel, not unlike our
huddle under the sugarcane. And I'd told her the truth: that
he'd asked me up to his room and that I intended to go. If she
was shocked, she didn't show it in her face. If she'd wondered
about my husband, she didn't ask. Perhaps those are the signposts. My cousin knew life was complicated and none of us
were fully who we pretended to be.

"But, Maydelis, what will you tell Ronny?" Jeanette slaps
a mosquito on her arm and leaves a streak of blood.

"That we drank too much. That I decided to stay in your
room. And I'll tell him the truth about this—that we decided
to leave to Varadero so you could see the beach."

"But he won't worry that he hasn't heard from you since
yesterday?"

"Sometimes I don't come home, Jeanette. Sometimes he
doesn't either."

There. The truth. It's out and engulfing us with the sticky
country air. Jeanette doesn't press me further. But I know
what she wants to know, so I add: "The sex was okay."

I don't add that he slipped me crisp euros "to buy some
new clothes since you didn't pack an overnight bag." That
something about seducing a man into offering his wallet
turned me on. That it didn't even matter who lay beneath
me—it was my own smell and heat and indecency that drove
me to orgasm. No, I don't say that I fantasized myself a full-
blown jinetera.

Not that it could be my life: the fantasy would end. My
skin is light, hair stringy straight. In Cuba, a white jinetera
selling sex goes hungry. It's the very young, very dark-skinned
women these men are after. Everyone knows this. There are
jokes even: *they didn't come here to see themselves.*

No, I wouldn't last as a jinetera. What I need is to leave,

earn some money, and come back. Buy stuff to sell here. I don't know.

———·———

The German, the anomaly, is in the driver's seat waiting when we get back.

"I was about to go looking for you two with a machete," he quips.

We finish our sandwiches while he drives. We sit silently, the three of us, and watch the rural townships go by. And when we reach a small town just miles from Cárdenas, El Alemán announces that he wants to buy liquor "before the expensive tourist places."

The three of us are a spectacle in this town of maybe two hundred. We walk the broken sidewalks and whole families rush to the windows of their homes to look us over. At the corner cafetería, the shelves are bare. This isn't La Habana with plenty of food and imports. The people here eye us carefully, and I can see them wondering what we have to offer. I'd be doing the same.

"Pinga, qué mierda," a man in a grubby undershirt says from a stool before the open-air counter. He's huddled over a small antenna television tuned to baseball in black and white, slamming its side.

"I haven't seen one of those in decades!" El Alemán says, turning to me with elation. I smile politely.

On the dirt road that traverses the main street of the town, a group of little girls stops jumping rope to look at us.

"He a Yuma?" one girl asks me. She can pick out the Cuban by sight. She's tiny but imposing, with a husky voice.

"Shut up, Adalisa," an older girl cautions. She holds the long telephone cord they've been using as a jump rope in one hand and places the other on her hip full of attitude.

"Where's the nearest store?" I ask the one called Adalisa.

"For what?" she responds, looking Jeanette up and down. A man passes on a bicycle and splatters my leg with mud.

"Rum."

She points toward the end of the block.

"I'll take you for a dollar," says her friend. We ignore them and keep going. Jeanette glances back at the children with such a sad smile that I look away in embarrassment.

The corner store is a wooden shack big enough for two people standing side by side. A description of goods and prices are hand-painted onto the side of the shack. The man on the other side of the iron bars watches us cautiously.

"Tell him I want three bottles of the best rum he's got. Havana Club," El Alemán says to me. "And no funny business. Tell him I can see the prices with my own eyes." I don't say so obviously. I just tell the man we want three bottles of Siete Años. He smiles. "Yuma knows his rum."

"Alemán," I correct him.

"Same shit," he responds.

When we get back to the car, it won't start. El Alemán turns and turns the key, and the engine just sputters.

"Are you kidding me?" he shouts. "What the fuck did these people do to the car?"

"What people?" I say, rolling down the window.

"Obviously one of the townspeople did something to my car."

"Why would they do that?" Jeanette says.

El Alemán turns the key again but the car just shakes.

"Of course they didn't do anything," I say.

"Don't you see? They're trying to rob us."

"Oh my God." Jeanette brings a hand to her mouth. "I hadn't even thought of that."

"That's absurd. Do you know how quickly the cops respond to tourist complaints?"

"Maydelis, it makes sense." Jeanette leans over from the back seat and places a hand on my arm. "But never mind, what do we do?"

I get out of the car and slam the door. I can hear Jeanette as I march through the dirt in my chancletas toward the cafetería, a long platform painted in peeling blue and surrounded by patches of grass. I hear Jeanette say, "Where is she going?"

The four men watching the baseball game gather around to hear my story. I'm the excitement for the day.

"Coño," a dark, thick man in rubber boots says. "Let me see if señora Lilia is around. She's the one with a phone. She lives ten minutes from here." He gets up from his stool.

"Wait," I say. "Let me get the German man. He's the one who should talk to the rental agency."

"Why, linda? You can talk to them in Spanish."

"No, no, he speaks English," I say. "The rental agency will speak English."

I feel the men watch me walk away. Certain towns like this feel frozen, like time functions differently, drips through an IV. I tap the driver's-side window, because El Alemán has locked himself into the car. He and Jeanette swelter, their faces shiny. El Alemán rolls down the window just a sliver.

"There's one phone in the town," I say. "Ten minutes from here in some lady's house. One of the townspeople will take us."

"Are you crazy, woman?" El Alemán shouts.

At this, Jeanette's eyes widen. I see her perk up. Her bracelets jangle as she crosses her arms.

"There is no way in hell I am going anywhere with one of those people," El Alemán says. "That's the setup, you see?

They did something to the car and now they'll lead us over to this 'phone,' and that's where they'll rob us." He glares in the direction of the cafetería. "Get in the fucking car," he says.

"No." A knot blooms in my chest.

"You don't have to talk to her like—" Now Jeanette looks angry.

"You have a better idea?" I say to El Alemán. His face is turning red, redder than its natural red.

I see Jeanette shift in her seat and bite a nail. She eyes El Alemán and then looks at me like she's trying to communicate something with her eyes. Her lips curl.

"Tell the Black one to go himself," El Alemán says. "Tell him to call a mechanic. Tell that worthless thief I'll give him a dollar and that's all he's getting from me."

Now Jeanette opens the door and comes to stand beside me. "Qué comemierda este viejo," she says in accented Spanish, and I try to stifle a laugh.

"You're going with her?" El Alemán says. "Well, I guess I'm the only one who values my life."

Jeanette ignores him. She takes my elbow as she did in the sugarcane field, only she's gripping me harder now. We start walking toward the cafetería.

The men have gone back to their baseball game. The whole town is silent, so different from La Habana. The only sound is the drone of the television.

"You really don't think someone did something to the car?" she asks when we're out of earshot.

"No," I say. "That's not how it works."

"How what works?"

"You make friends, not enemies, if what you're after is money."

"The Black one," it turns out, has a name. Reinaldo. He offers to take us to señora Lilia's house to use the phone. He walks with a long gait, arms swinging at his side, periodically wiping his face with a corner of his yellowed tank top and exposing his belly to us. He knows everyone we pass, and they yell greetings to one another. Some people ask him point-blank: Who are they? Why are they here?

I notice a change in Jeanette when El Alemán isn't with us. She slips more easily into Spanish, seems to swing her hips a little more loosely. She snaps back at the men who catcall with empty, bored faces, throws curses and friendly jabs right back at Reinaldo. I settle, relieved, into the role of participant, no longer the guide.

"But what's the problem, though?" Reinaldo says to Jeanette.

"Coño, how am I supposed to know? It just doesn't start."

"Pssssh," Reinaldo says through his teeth, gnashing on a cigar.

I feel the buzz of a mosquito at my neck and hope they won't make a feast of us by the time we leave. We turn right, following Reinaldo, onto a dirt path that runs between two Soviet-era complexes. Laundry swings from window to window, flapping in the dust, and chickens wander in and out of the building's entryway. I can see a couple faces through the iron bars of the windows.

"Why you wanna go with that viejo anyway?" Reinaldo says in my direction, but still looking at Jeanette. "You take me, I'll show you a good time. Got my own car and everything."

Jeanette starts to say something but I cut her off. "You gonna pay for the hotel?"

"Psssh," Reinaldo says again.

Once, Ronny and I went on vacation, staying at a beach house in Santa María del Mar, a reward from his boss for the best doctors. The house itself was falling apart. All night

I heard mice skittering along the walls and huge palmetto bugs flying in and out through holes along the baseboards. The beach, too, was far less appealing than the tourist beaches, which in those days were still off-limits to Cubans like us: murky water, garbage along the shore.

But Santa María del Mar is still my favorite memory of the two of us. Just an hour from home, we were unfamiliar friends again, hand in hand, sleeping naked in bed to escape the heat, the slow ceiling fan whipping my long hair over his chest in a steady, slow rhythm. *This is how most relationships must end,* I think. Slow and without drama or pandemonium, without reason: just two people who become accessories to the bland survival of the everyday.

When we returned to La Habana, a leak had ripped a chunk of plaster from the ceiling and it took us months to find the money and materials to fix it. Meanwhile there were buckets to catch water each time it rained and we stopped speaking of the nonessential. We wrote for money from Jeanette's mom in Miami to fix the hole in the ceiling. Then the sky was gone, and the house was dark again.

———

We get to the house with the phone. It's a squat, corrugated-roof hut surrounded by identical ones. There is a concrete porch, where an old woman with dark sunspots sits on a rocking chair, fanning herself. Bougainvillea vines snake around the house and blossom out into the sun.

"Señora Lilia," Reinaldo says.

The woman smiles and smooths her white hair. She introduces herself when I hand over a few coins for the phone call.

Jeanette offers to pay but she's carrying only divisa, not moneda nacional. Constantly she complains about the *un-*

fairness of the double-currency system, about how *mad* she feels paying a commission to exchange dollars into CUCs. There seem so many other easy injustices to point to; I'm frequently amused by what catches her fancy.

In Lilia's stuffy living room, packed to the brim with trinkets and religious figures, I dial the number on the rental car contract while Jeanette sits on the porch, smoking a cigarette with Reinaldo and pretending she doesn't notice him creeping in, flirtatious, going for the foreign kill. I watch them through the wooden slats filtering dusty light into Lilia's tiny living room. The whirr of a refrigerator reaches all the way to me, and I can't hear what Reinaldo and Jeanette are saying outside. The sheets hanging in place of doors inside the house rustle with a sudden breeze.

The rental agency, unsurprisingly, is less than helpful. It will take them hours, maybe four or five, says the high-pitched woman on the other end of the line. They don't have anyone, she explains, anywhere near us. She shouts questions at other people in the office, whom I can hear only through muffled replies. Yes, four to five hours, she confirms. I give them an approximate address, and the woman laughs. "En casa del carajo," she says.

Outside, Lilia has joined Reinaldo and Jeanette. They are doubled in laughter, some joke I've missed.

"It's going to take all day," I announce, puncturing the group's joy with bad news.

Jeanette looks troubled, Reinaldo unsurprised. Lilia is bored again, fanning herself.

We decide on a plan: We will go back to the car, and on the way, Reinaldo will stop by the house of his buddy who, he says, "can fix anything from a TV antenna to a rocket ship." His buddy will see if he can get the car running. I will distract

El Alemán somehow. Or bear his anger and paranoia, hoping he doesn't insult Friend of Reinaldo and leave us to the rental agency, which, I predict, will take double their time estimate. We set off after kissing Lilia goodbye.

We pass the apartment complex again. We step from the dirt road onto the sidewalk that crosses the whole small town, walk under the shade of sprawling trees and past empty stores, wave hello to a man on horseback dragging a cart full of vegetables. We answer questions from a few nosy townspeople. See the girls jumping rope again.

It's all so familiar, but then midway back, Jeanette surprises me.

"What if," she says, glancing away from Reinaldo and lowering her voice, "we pay someone to drive us instead? What if we run off and leave El Alemán?"

I think she's joking, so I laugh, shield my eyes from the sun, and kick away the branches along our path as a red-skinned dog wanders by our side, scratching itself.

"I'm serious," she says. "What do we need him for?"

The dog's rib cage is outlined like a dental impression. It looks up with droopy, sad eyes.

"Don't you remember? He was going to pay," I say, "for the hotel in Varadero. It's expensive."

"Psshhh," Jeanette says, sounding like Reinaldo in a way that annoys me. "We don't really need to go to Varadero anyways. Isn't it just full of tourists?"

"Yeah, and beautiful beach." I want to say that she *is* a tourist but hold my tongue. "Where would we go if we don't go to Varadero? Back to La Habana?"

"You don't want that, do you?"

Ahead of us, Reinaldo shoos the dog away. I look up at the sun filtering through the branches of a tree until my eye

squints of its own volition. I think of Ronny playing dominoes on the promenade in front of our house in Playa. I think
of the hole in the ceiling, which still leaks even though he
"fixed" it. I think of Ronny in his checkered shirt with a
Bucanero in hand, arguing loudly with passersby for hours.

"No, I don't," I say.

"What about Camagüey?" Jeanette says. "I always
wanted to see Grandma Dolores's house."

I swallow hard and look at the orange outline of dirt on
my white sandals. Something has ruptured on the car ride
here. Maybe something ruptured long before that. *Fuck it,*
I think, picturing El Alemán receding in the background,
picturing my husband. Wondering if I'd have to send Ronny
money from Miami. How else would he agree to a divorce?
And knowing the truth though I won't let myself near it: I'm
probably never leaving—not the country, not Ronny. But
I need the fantasy. I need the made-up plans. *Auf Wieder-
sehen,* Germany. *Adiós.*

"What about Santa María del Mar for a few hours and
then Abuela Dolores's house?" I say.

She smiles and takes my hand. "A beach is a beach, no?"

I feel shivers of exhilaration, an exhilaration I'd felt the
night before, convulsing man beneath me, shouting my name
like he worshipped at my feet. The rest is easy.

Jeanette offers Reinaldo more money than he'll see in
months, fifty or sixty US dollars. We offer to fill his tank too.
I don't know the address of the beach house, but Reinaldo
knows how to get to Santa María del Mar and I'm familiar
with the area. I'm nervous, but I tell El Alemán the rental
agency has someone on the way. It's not a lie, and that makes
me feel better. I tell him Jeanette and I are going in search
of a bathroom and need our bags to freshen up. He tells us

we're asking for trouble, and I wonder if he means murder or rape or something else entirely. I don't wait long enough to find out.

Reinaldo, Jeanette, and I turn the corner past the cafetería, and I glance back at the rental car, stout and red, in the middle of a barren field like a miniature barn house in all those US movies. I see El Alemán shading his eyes and looking small. We run. We run in the direction of Reinaldo's house two blocks away and hop into his car. Then the wind is whipping at my face again and all the island feels like a blur.

9

PEOPLE LIKE THAT

Jeanette
Camagüey, 2015

We are sitting in rocking chairs by the front door, open to a field of guava bushes, when a man arrives. My grandmother introduces him as her neighbor; he says he heard she had a visitor from the United States. He is my age and Black. My grandmother squints her eyes when he speaks, but I can't read her response. Maydelis seems uninterested in the man. She stubs her filterless cigarette, the ones offered at the bodega, and leaves for the kitchen without saying a word to him. The man wears red skinny jeans, a red-and-white polo shirt. He has a kind of mohawk buzz cut. I follow Maydelis to the kitchen to fetch the visitor a beer because that seems like the thing to do.

"Repartero," she says. Maydelis settles at the little kitchen table beside the ancient stove and pulls out another cigarette. She sucks hungrily and blows delicate wisps and I wonder where the rest of the smoke goes, does it just sit inside her?

"Don't you see how he dresses, his fake-diamond earrings?" she says.

"Repartero?" I repeat and she sighs.

I've been in Cuba only a week, but I sense she is tiring of me. She spent days guiding me all over La Habana, answering my questions like a mother explaining the basic ways of the world to a child. She has brought me to this tiny town in Camagüey, to the campo, to meet my grandmother, but I sense she'd rather be anywhere else. All she wants to talk about is the United States, what it's like *over there*. I do not tell her I have come to visit Cuba because I have nothing left *over there*. That I am *over there*'s worst representative.

"A repartero is a kind of person," Maydelis says. "They dress like reggaeton stars. They have no class, if you know what I mean. They talk bad."

I do not know what she means, but she lists kinds of people that exist in Cuba—freakies, emos, Mickeys, repas. She lists what they wear and what music they listen to and where they hang out and I realize every country is different but the same. Every country has its own lunch tables. I open the massive ice box, shuffle past slabs of mamey and fruta bomba, cheese wrapped in wet cloth, until my hand reaches a cold Cristal. I can sense Maydelis wants to say more, but I leave her in the kitchen because I am curious about the visitor. I am more curious about the visitor than "kinds of people."

When I hand the beer to him, my grandmother wiggles in her chair and settles back. The man smiles at me, and my grandmother is not unfriendly but she does not smile.

"I have horses," the man says to me. His name is Yosmany, he says. "I have two."

He says it like a question and my grandmother and the man look at me like they expect a response.

"Horses?" I say. The sun is setting and the mosquitoes are out in full force. I slap one on my thigh and it sticks to my skin, a tiny carcass.

"You want to ride one?" Yosmany asks. Something about the way he smiles reminds me of Mario and I feel the familiar gut punch, the craving.

"No," my grandmother answers for me. "It is dark. She does not want to ride one."

"But I do," I say. "I want to ride a horse."

Yosmany smiles and I want to lick his teeth.

My grandmother takes a long breath and places a hand on the cane that leans against her rocking chair. "Maybe tomorrow." She turns to Yosmany. "We are busy catching up. I have not known this granddaughter of mine in her twenty-eight years. Plus we go to sleep early."

"Coño, Abuela," says Yosmany, and it bothers me that he calls her grandmother, because I have just gained possession of her for the first time. I am not ready to share.

"How's La Yuma?" Yosmany asks, looking at me. "Is it everything they say?"

I start to answer but my grandmother cuts me off again. Some moments I want her closer, and then my feelings flicker, switch. I grow annoyed. I think of Maydelis's mom, my tía Elena, saying that all her life my mother acted like she didn't belong in the family, had been born into a family beneath her. That she spent all her time in her room and often exploded in anger at my grandmother over any little thing. And then I kind of feel it too, that maybe I was wrong to think there was something here for me, a recognizable piece of me.

"I *wish* this country would become completely capitalist," my grandmother says as if exhaling smoke. "I wish it would. Then you would see what capitalism *really* is. You kids, you have no idea because you didn't see it. You'll see what it really is."

"Coño, Abuela," Yosmany says again.

"I am tired. I'd like to go to bed now." My grandmother

folds her fan in her lap. It depicts colonial scenes, women in hoop skirts and their gallant men.

"Pero don't get mad, Abuela," Yosmany says.

———·———

When he leaves, my grandmother's cat Theo jumps onto my lap. He has a piece of lace in his mouth, and she has no idea where it came from.

I stole a lacy thong once. In high school, I walked into a Victoria's Secret and stuck it in my pocket. The clerk who caught me was named Victoria, which cracked me up. My mother fetched me from a room behind the store, where a security guard lorded over me, eyes on my cleavage. He "let me off easy."

My mother chastised me with a speech about Cuba. "Do you know," she said, "that people buy steak from a food vendor on the side of the road? They think it is steak, because it is glossy. It looks juicy.

"Do you know," she said, "that they bite into the steak and they think, oh, this is a tough steak, and they don't think, this is a mango peel—they don't think, this is a mopping rag charred, marinated, blood-orange-soaked, a mopping rag resembling meat. Of course they don't think this is a mopping rag masquerading as meat.

"Do you know," she said, "that there are no cats in Cuba? Think about that, Jeanette, no cats. Where do you think all the cats have gone, do you think they just disappeared overnight?

"Jeanette," she said, "I came here to freedom so you'd never have to steal."

That is what I am thinking as I pet my grandmother's cat: I am thinking about a thong. I am thinking about stores and stories and stealing. It is 2015. Things are different in Cuba in 2015. I don't know if my grandmother ate mopping-rag steak during the Special Period. If that ever even existed. I don't know if she had another cat when the Soviets fell—what was it, 1989? But it is 2015 now, and my grandmother is round and portentous, nothing like my mother. She is eighty-something in a sleeveless housedress. Each time she emphasizes a word with a swipe of her arm, it jiggles like custard. Her voice, too, sprawls, coats everything like dust. Her eyes punctuate: large in delight, slanted when her statements sharpen.

"Jeanette," she says as if she reads my thoughts, "don't believe the mercenary media—we struggle, but we are happy here." *Squint, slant.*

Maydelis has left the kitchen and joined us again by the doorway, waiting for a breeze. She rolls her eyes but my grandmother can't see her. I've heard Maydelis rant about how she is frustrated here. I know how she feels.

Abuela makes coffee even though outside it is dark as the chicory-laced grounds. She tells Maydelis that Yosmany invited me to ride his horse, and Maydelis snorts.

"Don't be silly, Jeanette," she says, scrunching her hair into a fat pouf atop her head. "He just wants to woo you so you can whisk him off to La Yuma. Or he will spend all evening riding horses with you and then ask for a pair of sneakers and an iPhone, ha ha ha."

Maydelis had asked me for a pair of sneakers, but I don't mention that. I brought her a pair of Nikes tucked in one of those fifty-pound canvas bags the Cubans call *gusanos*. Gusanos are worms. Back in the Cold War days, they called Cubans who left the country for Miami gusanos. I, daughter of a worm.

"You can't trust Black men," my grandmother says, and I nearly choke on my cafecito.

This I still haven't gotten used to, the blatant racism, how it commingles with revolutionary fervor at times in the older generation in a way that seems unlikely. But perhaps I am naïve and racism among even revolutionaries is as obvious as me sticking a lacy thong in my pocket at sixteen. As obvious as the fact that I am no good.

I say nothing.

I want to love my grandmother, but my mother has poisoned me. She said once my grandmother loved her country more than her blood. She said my grandmother was a murderous devotee of a regime. She said I could never speak to my grandmother.

My mother slapped me when I said I loved Che Guevara's *Motorcycle Diaries,* when I said Fidel Castro was handsome in his youth. My mother told me I should never go to Cuba until That Man is dead, she wouldn't see me to the airport. I know that she likes me here only because there is no heroin here. I know that she likes me here because Suboxone has failed me once already.

And me? What am I doing here? I thought Cuba could be some kind of connective tissue, maybe even show me my mother. Make a piece of her make sense. I remember pressing her about why she left as the girl, Ana, watched cartoons last year, as my mother let me fail yet another person. Or perhaps I just needed somewhere to run to in this moment and only Cuba felt faintly familiar. There is no Meaning here. Only questions.

I want to love my grandmother, but she is blank faced, spreading rice on her splintered kitchen table, picking out the black kernels and the grit. Crooked arthritic fingers, tight-lipped and unsmiling face. I want to love her but it is too quiet in this house.

But it isn't as though Black Cubans fare better in Miami, where racism is just slightly more polite, a little quieter. This is fact: In Miami, *Cuban* is synonymous with *white*. In Miami, Cubans will scoff when you call them Latino. "I'm not Latino, I'm Cuban," they will say. By which they mean, *I am white, another kind of white you don't know about, outsider.*

I was ignorant. In high school, I saw a documentary about the Buena Vista Social Club, and before that I hadn't known there were many Black Cubans. And then I asked my mother, "How come there are so many Black Cubans in Cuba and so few in Miami or are there more but they live somewhere else?" and she looked at me like the question wasn't a question at all but bordered on insult. (Don't ask my mother about her curly hair. Don't ask my mother about some of her features. Don't ask her why she hates to tan.)

I say nothing to my grandmother. Maydelis talks about how she wishes she could travel, maybe even live somewhere else for just a little while, so she could make some money to bring back to Cuba, or maybe just get a visa to visit so she could buy stuff to sell. She reiterates for the millionth time that the average salary for a Cuban government employee is ten dollars a month. "*Ten dollars!*" she says.

My grandmother pays Maydelis no mind. She cuts her off. "I know you're probably wondering about your mother and me, Jeanette," my grandmother says, abruptly.

Another fact: I want to look as effortless as these women. It isn't until Cuba that I realize how uncomfortable I am in my neatness. It seems to me the classier the outfit, the more it hides. I am neat and a thief, recovering from a substance-use disorder, a term I didn't know until rehab. Straight out the airport, in La Habana, I marveled at the women in their tiny sequined jeans shorts, their bra tops that exposed dimpled stomachs. Effortless. *Here I am in all my imperfection, motherfuckers,* their sweat-glistened skin proclaimed. Maydelis in her bootleg polo shirt. My grandmother in a satin housedress, her cone-shaped bra peeking through the armholes, her cone-shaped bra barely containing the skin that seeps over its elastic.

"I know it's about politics, Abuela," I say. "I don't care about that."

"It is sad," she says, "that I haven't spoken to her since she left. It is sad that I didn't know you until now."

Maydelis exhales a wisp, sucks an ocean. "Very sad," she adds.

I flap my fan. Flap, flap, flap. Then I set it down. "She doesn't know I'm here," I say after a long pause. "I mean she knows I'm here, in Cuba, but she doesn't know I came to see you."

"Will you tell her?" Maydelis asks.

One thing I notice: fewer women in Cuba wear makeup. Some women preen in jewelry and heels, sequins and bangles, and a bare face. Not all, but many. It is too hot, probably. But I am not here to draw conclusions or take answers home. I know everyone will say in Miami, *Tell me about Cuba*. Most of them expecting an answer like, *It is hell on earth*. Or maybe a few, subversively, will ask me expecting an answer like, *It is socialist paradise*. I'd rather answer with a question, *Tell me about the United States?*

"It's complicated," I say.

"So sad," Abuela says.

So my mother hates her mother. There are times I thought I hated my mother, so I understand, though I wonder if only politics divided them. I grew up in Miami, yes, and watched family dinners devolve into all-out brawls over mere mention of Cuba-anything, but I am as uninterested in the familiar arguments as my cousin Maydelis, also my age. We grew up on opposite shores but equally drenched in the political, in living everything through the context of a country miles away. I understand her fatigue. I, too, am tired.

———·———

Maydelis and I stay up talking after my grandmother has gone to bed. We sit on plastic chairs in the hallway, which is lined with sepia photos and a termite-ridden bookcase that holds ancient-looking hardcover books. They'd be at home in any grand library, the kind where rolling ladders reach the highest volumes and portraits of old dead white men line the walls.

I ask Maydelis about the books and she shrugs, says, "They're just books." But I pick one up and then another, amazed at their fragility. The two oldest-looking ones are enclosed in plastic. I take one out of its wrapping and marvel at the crinkling, disintegrating pages. CECILIA VALDÉS, O LA LOMA DEL ÁNGEL, reads the cover in embossed, faded gold. CIRILO VILLAVERDE. I flip the yellowed pages carefully until I find the date of printing: 1839. I gasp. Maydelis barely looks over.

The next is *Les Misérables* by Victor Hugo, a Spanish translation. It is harder to find a date in that one but from the delicate, humidity-beaten pages, the type so faded it is barely legible, it's obvious that the book could be a contemporary to *Cecilia Valdés*. I flip its pages and notice something scrawled in the margin, in black ink turned wispy gray, ornate script. I bring my face closer but can make out only the last word, *fuerza*. Force.

I've been sober almost a year—fuck whoever says Suboxone doesn't count—but still find myself making calculations like *How much Oxy could I buy if I sold an antique book, a rare collectible?* But then I remember that even if I'm not getting high, I still need money. Money my mother won't give me anymore. Money my temp jobs hardly pay me. My mother would pay for a trip to Cuba but wouldn't see me to the airport. My mother would pay for a trip to Cuba but would check my eyes each time I said I needed help buying groceries.

"Maydelis, these are incredible. Where did they come from?" I ask her.

"They were in the wall."

I stare at her.

"Abuela found them in the walls of the house—twenty years ago, I'm talking about—when she was expanding the house."

I have heard this rumor, about valuable artifacts hiding behind the innocuous-looking plaster of homes all over Cuba, though I've heard only of jewels, gold, old bills now worthless; I've never heard of old books hidden in the walls. I have also, perhaps, assumed the story was just another exaggeration, another drama-seeped tale from my mother.

My mother's story was that in the 1950s and '60s, when wealthy Cuban families plotted escape from the revolution, they sometimes hid their valuables in the walls of their homes. Back then, these wealthy families expected the revolution to fail—a year or two sunbathing in Miami, a year or two playing dominoes and staring at the ocean. Some later immigrants were allowed to leave the country with only two changes of clothing and three pairs of underwear. That was my mother.

Any money or jewelry left behind, which the families were forbidden to take out of the country, would become property of the state. But these families, expecting to return to the island soon enough to reclaim their property and resume their wealthy lives, buried treasure in their sprawling yards, hid jewels in the foundation of their mansions, stacked cash beneath the floorboards. There were stories of some of these once-opulent homes in those once-elite neighborhoods of La Habana crumbling to ruins around the families now living in them, families whose bad luck turned once they saw sparkling rubies and sapphires beckoning in the rubble.

"Maydelis, this is incredible," I say once more.

"I know," she says, but she doesn't seem to think it's incredible at all.

———·———

I steal the book in the middle of the night. My grandmother and Maydelis are asleep. Crickets chirp and flies buzz in and out of the wooden-slat windows. So easy. I tiptoe through the hallway, grab *Les Misérables* off the shelf, take it to my room, and tuck it into a corner of my gusano beneath some shirts.

In the confines of the room—my grandmother's room, which she has given up for me, the visitor—I lie spread-eagle and watch the blades of a painfully slow fan waltz above me. I tell myself it is okay, no one will notice, that someday I will be in a better financial position and I will come back to Cuba. I will give my grandmother, my cousin, all my family whatever money the book was worth times a hundred. I wonder what an antiques dealer might pay for a rare book, how many bills that money might cover, how much rent, how many nights without sweat rolling down my forehead and into my already damp pillow. I miss the air-conditioning of my apartment in Miami. I have hated that apartment at every turn, but now I miss it. That apartment with its peeling paint and moldy bathroom, the only place I could afford after my mother cut me off.

In the morning, I wake before my grandmother and Maydelis and make them coffee. They are amused that a Yumita like me can make good espresso on the disintegrating stovetop. My grandmother gives me seeds for the rooster and chickens and guanajos, and I walk through the dirt spreading the bounty like a flower girl at the altar. Maydelis takes advantage of the hens' commotion to search for eggs. She tells me she loves it here, a break from La Habana's commotion. I miss that commotion. I spent only a week in La Habana before arriving to this town with her to visit our grandmother. We fry the eggs, yolks violently red from the ateje seeds.

I tell myself there are more books where *Les Misérables* came from. I tell myself no one will even notice that one book missing. I tell myself that, really, I am doing my grandmother a favor. She has no idea how valuable those books might be, and moths will surely eat them or hurricanes whip them away. It is a miracle they have survived even this long. I am saving one of the books, ensuring its place in the world, because something so precious needs a place in the world.

When my grandmother notices the book missing, I've been in Camagüey for another week. Each day has bled into the next, endless porch rocking, endless walks on dirt roads, endless visits from curious neighbors who, even miles away, learn of my arrival.

My grandmother simply walks into the kitchen one morning as I sit peeling a mamey and says, no hint of anger or emotion, "El negro stole one of my books."

"What?" I say, a current running through me.

"*Les Misérables.* I had a book, an original printing of the Spanish version. A rare book worth money."

I am taken aback though I suppose there is no reason my grandmother shouldn't know this. I am hit once again, like so many times on this trip, with truth that doesn't square with my notions of Cuba or Cubans. There is an interest in rare collections! And why shouldn't there be? I assumed such aesthetic pleasures would not interest Cubans, who surely have more concrete matters to attend to, more utilitarian purchases to pine for, even to notice a valuable antique relic tucked in a dust-engulfed bookshelf. It seems another naïve notion to me now. I feel like a clumsy tourist making sense of a world that feels my own emotionally but clearly is not.

"It is a special book. Something that had been in our family for ages. A gift from my great-grandmother. You know I hid it in the wall for years, that's how special it is? And now he took it."

More that I can't make sense of. Maydelis said that my grandmother found it in the wall. She didn't say my grandmother was the one who put it there in the first place. Was my grandmother wealthy once, and had she wanted to leave too? It doesn't square with her politics. Nothing makes sense.

"Why would you assume he took it, Abuela?" I say, sliding the blunt knife away from me and placing the mamey on the table.

"Who else?" she says. "Yesterday I went to the bathroom and nobody watched him in the living room. That negro knows more than you'd think looking at him."

Maydelis comes in with a plastic bag of bread my grandmother sent for from a neighbor who works at a bakery. She looks at both our faces and sets the bag down. Sweat has formed an outline of her spine through her tank top. She asks what's going on and my grandmother repeats her accusation. Maydelis's eyes shift to me and I look down at the fruit on the table. My heart races. I feel cold even as I sit in the unmoving hot air.

"I will report him," my grandmother says. "I will report

him to the Comité. I will report him to his workplace. I will even call the police."

"Wait, wait," Maydelis says. "Let me talk to him first."

"Are you out of your mind?" My grandmother places a hand on the table to steady herself. She breathes hard.

"Sit," I say, getting up and guiding my grandmother toward my chair. I still don't dare look at Maydelis.

"I—think I can reason with him, Abuela. I won't go alone," Maydelis says. "Jeanette will go with me. Let us try that first at least."

"You can't trust people like that," my grandmother says, placing a hand over the knife I have discarded. "If they don't do it on the way in, they do it on the way out."

I have heard that racist Cuban expression from my mother so many times.

My grandmother turns to face me. "Do you see what Cuba is becoming?"

———

I decide to avoid Maydelis until the moment of our walk to Yosmany's house. I wonder if she really intends to go, or if she plans to confront me. For hours I hole up in my room and pretend to nap. I creep to the door to listen for bits of conversation but I hear nothing about the book or about the neighbor. When I do leave the bedroom, there is no one in the hall.

So I slip the book from my bag and place it back on the bookshelf in its original enclosure, where two books now slant toward the void. I consider saying I just borrowed it, I wanted to read it, but it's too late for that. Besides, my grandmother and Maydelis know I can barely read Spanish.

I scour my hands as if I can wash away the ugliness eating at me. I scrub and scrub until my hands are raw, and I remember that water comes every other day here in the campo, that my grandmother doesn't have a tank to store extra gallons, as Maydelis does in her home in La Habana.

When I leave the bathroom, Maydelis stands in the hallway, looking at me. Her hair is plastered to her wet forehead. She wears tiny shorts and flip-flops. One hand is on her hip in that very Cuban back-of-the-hand pose that betrays her real emotion. "I guess Abuela didn't look too carefully at the bookshelf," she says, not taking her eyes off me.

"What do you mean?" I can hear the catch in my own voice.

"The book is there."

"Oh," I turn my back to her, already heading to my room. "That's good news then. We don't have to look for Yosmany."

"Yeah," she says. "Good news for Yosmany."

I almost add, *And Abuela*—but I can't bring myself to say it.

I can hear her, Abuela Dolores, humming to herself in the kitchen. She is making my favorite, fricasé de pollo. Maydelis and I will return to La Habana tomorrow. Then a few more days and I fly back to Miami. And for no real reason, what I think about in that moment is that photo that came out in some of the Miami newspapers a little while back, Fidel Castro's son Fidelito, beaming, a beard like his father's, arms around Paris Hilton and Naomi Campbell at some grand celebration or other in La Habana.

How far away that glamour feels from the campo, not so much in an economic sense but because news is slower, time trickles. There are luxury stores that sell Versace to tourists in La Habana now, but here oxen still till the land and my grandmother just wants a place to buy cumin that isn't a flight away. She says cumin has disappeared.

"It was me," I say to Maydelis, and all we can hear is my grandmother's humming.

"I know," she whispers, and I wait for her to ask me why but she doesn't. I wait for her to ask why so I can confess that I think there is nothing I will ever be good at and no way that I will ever make up for the person I've been.

"You know," Maydelis says, fanning herself, "I thought after this—after we'd met each other for the first time like this and spent all this time together like this—I thought you might send for me. I might try for a visa. I thought you would help me like that, but I realize now you wouldn't. You wouldn't do that for me."

"Of course I would!" I say, but she is right and I am stunned. I want to say that it's not so easy, that I am a screwed-up recovering addict who lives in a moldy apartment and that I can barely support myself, much less someone else, and I almost, almost want to say, *It's not that bad here,* but then I know she's liable to ask me why I don't stay then—and I don't have an answer.

She walks away. Pulls a cigarette pack from her back pocket and leaves through the door.

I start to follow, but my grandmother sidles up beside me with a spoonful of the chicken stew, blowing over it. "Prueba," she says, and sticks the spoon in my mouth.

I can taste the tomato, garlic, onion, the cumin she's just run out of. The fricasé burns my tongue, but I say, delicious.

She takes my hand and leads me to the kitchen. We pass the bookshelf. "I shouldn't have assumed Yosmany took it," my grandmother says, turning to me, and I know that Cuba belongs to me even less than I ever believed.

I say nothing, but I pick up the book again and it feels heavier than before. I turn to the page with the faint ink and hold it up to the light as she watches me.

We are force, the ink reads in perfect script. Such an inscrutable thing to write in a book.

I look at my grandmother and think, *I am forced to love you.* But then, *You are forced to love me too.*

In the kitchen, we sit and wait for the hours to pass. Maydelis joins when she's finished smoking. The goats are bleating outside, and I can hear two people shouting in the distance. I can't tell if they are fighting, or joking and laughing. The kitchen smells like cumin and something else, something I can't identify, something ancient.

10

THAT BOMBS WOULD RAIN

Dolores
Camagüey, 1959

The day before Daniel Hernández killed a man for the first time, his two-year-old daughter learned to say *coffee*. She sat in the wooden high chair that he built himself, and Dolores had just placed the cafetera on the stove and turned up the gas. Little Elena wiggled her hands in the air. She said, "Mamá, café!" except she couldn't pronounce her *f*'s yet, so it sounded more like *cah-weh*.

Dolores laughed. Daniel laughed. He readied for work cutting caña as Dolores served three little cups of espresso: for her, Daniel, and their older daughter, seven-year-old Carmen. Dolores dipped her pinky into her cup and placed it in Elena's mouth. The toddler latched on to the tip of her mother's finger—Dolores had weaned her last year, but the little mouth didn't forget how to suckle with abandon. Elena, true Cuban, loved coffee at two years old.

Daniel's political convictions had emerged only a couple of years before. At first, Dolores feared the outcome. But as Daniel grew angrier in those years, she longed for those moments he'd sit on a stool in one corner of their two-room house, too busy fiddling with the radio dials to pay much attention to her. Radio Rebelde, the underground channel, consumed him. It originally broadcast out of Oriente, hours from Camagüey, but the rebels had set up satellite stations. Daniel kept the volume low, so the neighbors wouldn't hear, but Dolores caught snippets as she toiled around the house. Rebels and resistance, Cuba awakening, the people joining the *movement*.

Maybe in the Sierra Maestra. In her town in Camagüey, things were quieter. Rural Camagüey's news: that Carmen had slashed her finger with a scissor while cutting paper dolls out of newspaper, that Elena spilled black beans and rice all over the floor. Exhausted. Dolores feared what everyone feared—President Batista's men coming in the night, knocking down their door. President Batista's men with hands over her girls' mouths, President Batista's men demanding she dig her own grave. She knew the stories. She knew how fast an entire family disappeared in the night, dissipated like vapor. She knew how easily someone could erase her, knew she barely existed at all.

But to reason with Daniel. She'd whispered her concerns one night as they lay in bed and thick rain lulled them to false calm. How quick he had knocked her to the floor, said she probably wanted to open her legs for Batista, slashed the belt across her face so that a welt formed diagonally from the bottom of her left lip to her right eyebrow. She feared her husband more than any president or his men.

The day before Daniel Hernández killed a man for the first time, the guerrillero Fidel Castro made a plea from the mountains: Come with your rifles, your machetes, it's time. That's all it took. Daniel grabbed his straw hat and the blade he used to cut cane on his patrón's farm. Dolores didn't know how long he'd be gone or if he'd live. Just a few days of missed work meant she would have to feed the girls whatever was ripe on their little plot—some boiled plantains or malanga or, worse, a handful of nísperos, glasses of sugar water.

The day before Daniel Hernández killed a man for the first time, Dolores watched him leave down the dirt road behind their house. He hitched a ride, waved back once. Elena slept in Dolores's arms. Carmen grabbed her hand and yelled. She asked where her father was off to, work? Dolores lied and said he was visiting family. Carmen demanded to know when he'd be back. Daniel wore the same clothes he wore each day he worked the fields, left the same way he left each morning. But somehow Carmen sensed a different current to today's departure. Perhaps Dolores too eager to wave goodbye.

She told Carmen she could miss school that day. The girl quieted.

And, aside from no money for food, how nice to have the house to themselves. Dolores swept and dusted, mended Carmen's school clothes, knocked down ripe bananas with a wooden plank.

Later, they took a bus to the capital of the province. Carmen stood on the vinyl seat, nose glued to the window, and Elena wailed in Dolores's arms before collapsing into sleep. At the plaza, Dolores let the girls run free, Carmen dangling over the edge of the fountain, wiggling ripples into the water, Elena toddling at Dolores's feet. Dolores had no plan, no reason to be in the city. The best kind of feeling, to do something for no reason. She wanted to scream, wanted to dangle over the fountain like her daughter, force miniature waves with her fists.

That day was a Tuesday, a workday, and she watched bankers and shop owners wander through the plaza, watched the society women with their fancy prams and stockinged children, their nannies trailing behind. She knew her children looked feral in comparison—dirty and darker and poor. But she didn't care. Bolero, mambo, son: she could dance if she wanted. Through the alleys, between market vendors, in the parks, at every stoplight. As she used to do with Daniel before the children. At the huge church that anchored the plaza, two bells rang to announce the hour while on the steps a woman begged for change.

"Why is that woman sitting like that?" Carmen asked. She had run to the bench where Dolores sat. She caught her breath with a dramatic gulp.

"Children don't ask questions," Dolores said. "Don't leave your sister behind."

Elena sat on the concrete at the foot of the fountain, watching the women who click-clacked past in bell-shaped skirts and cat-eye glasses, a chicness that immediately separated the plaza women from campo women like Dolores who, no matter how much they washed, always wore a sheen and scent of dust and earth.

Dolores stayed until sunset, stayed until her stomach grumbled and the girls began to whine and cry. She paid the last few cents she had left besides bus fare for cucuruchos de maní from the plaza vendor, which quieted the girls long enough for the ride home.

Was she disappointed when Daniel found his way back three days later? Truthfully, yes. They were hungry. She'd desperately looked for work but every person she approached turned her away. Nobody wanted a two-year-old on their farm or in their factory, and with all four grandparents dead, she had no one to watch Elena.

But she had also never watched the hours unfold as when Daniel was gone, time offering up its bounty like the yuca she dug from the ground. Dolores did as she wanted. Dolores visited neighborhood women and crocheted on their porches, took long walks with her girls and ate plump guavas straight from the bush. Dolores forgot to check the time, had no need to ready anything for anyone at any specific moment, just the food they'd eat. She even listened to the radio—*her* radio now—and danced to Beny Moré and Bola de Nieve as she swept.

Daniel arrived grizzled, dirty, in borrowed fatigues too big for his frame. "I'm so hungry," he said as he walked through the door.

Carmen cried out, ran to his side.

"There's nothing," Dolores said. "I had no money for the market." Dolores readied herself for a reaction, but Daniel only stared and slumped into a chair.

"Two days ago," he said, "I killed a man."

"Not in front of the children," was all Dolores said. She knew Daniel didn't offer conversation as an invitation. He said what he wanted to say, and she listened. In that way, Dolores did as she cautioned her children to do.

Did she wish, some nights later, that events had reversed? Daniel killed by the military approaching from behind, undetected, deep in the Sierra? Did she wish never to know what happened to her husband, to say, *He disappeared into the mountains one day and I never saw him again—he is a martyr*? Not all nights.

Only the nights when Daniel came home rum-drenched, cursing the Yankee imperialists who paid him pennies while they cavorted with go-go girls in private clubs, when he dropped pesos, barely enough for milk, much less meat, into Dolores's hand.

The blows came fast—to the face, the stomach, Dolores's back. He'd lock the girls in their room. Carmen was old enough to hear her father's yelling, her mother's crying, but she stayed silent behind that door. Though Daniel had never touched the girls, they feared him, too, with a confused admiration that Dolores had possessed for her own violent father.

After the blows came kicks sometimes. With mud-caked boots. Drawing blood from a broken nose that never repaired right, from split lips and knocked-out teeth. She should have feared death but she didn't. In the moments when Daniel appeared ready to kill her, all thought ceased, and she retracted into the shell of her arms, saw splinters of light, spinning walls, felt like a child on a merry-go-round thrust off and ready to hit the floor. Sometimes, at the crescent of raw fear, she felt free, like she soared. The pain came later.

Some men apologized afterward. She had enough friends with husbands who "got a little out of hand sometimes," too, to know as much. Some men bought gifts and promised change. Daniel spared her that confusion, at least. Hours later, days later, in his sobriety, Daniel would say nothing of his violence. He'd ignore the bruises or the cuts, the bandages and homemade splints because they couldn't afford a doctor. He'd pat his girls on the head and bring them wildflowers that he hid in his pockets. If there was any conversation, it was about the news on the radio. *Freedom is coming,* he would say. *Inevitable.* He didn't mention a return to the mountains, though Dolores willed it those nights, willed it so hard.

But Daniel didn't mention joining the fight again. He still crouched with his ear to the radio each night. He still looked out each morning toward the field before him as if the Movement would come marching through darkness right to his door. But he had settled back into work and Dolores had settled back into her previous routine. Perhaps it had all been a phase, Daniel the hero.

His absence, though, had given Dolores ideas. She knew that it was no longer preposterous that a woman might leave her husband. There was even a woman, just a few miles away—a woman with two kids and no husband. The woman lived with her mother, sister, and sister's husband. And sure, people whispered about her, and some families didn't even want their kids mingling with hers, but the woman managed. She showed her face at the market and at school to pick up her children. She held birthday parties and invited Carmen.

Dolores knew, too, that once Carmen got older and Elena started school, she could leave the older girl in charge of the younger one and find work more easily. Maybe it was a matter of biding her time. She began to prepare. She hid little bits of her grocery allowance in a slit she cut under the mattress. She loosened a slat of wood from a wall and hid her most valuable possession there—an original printing of *Les Misérables* given to her by her grandmother Cecilia when she was a child. She started teaching Carmen how to cook simple dishes and put her in charge of little chores like dusting the furniture. And she befriended a neighborhood woman who owned a typewriter. She joined her every few days for coffee and to practice memorizing the keystrokes. The woman thought her simply curious and didn't mind showing off her prize possession. Dolores joined the woman's circle of friends who met each day at noon.

Daniel seemed to notice the change. Perhaps she lowered her head a little less or spoke a little more. Whatever it was, the new Dolores sharpened Daniel's wrath. A month after killing a man for the first time, Daniel broke three of Dolores's ribs and they had to borrow money to get Dolores to a hospital. She spent weeks in a rigid cast, and Carmen picked up more household chores.

By then, it was no longer just Daniel with his ear to the radio, whispering that, yes, an ouster of Batista might be possible. Dolores heard it even from the neighborhood women. Voices lowered, everyone leaning in, talk over coffee.

"—students in the capital who stormed the presidential palace."

"—five guerrilleros. Just boys, still baby-faced. Lined up against a wall and shot in the head one by one—"

Typewriter click.

"I heard the americanos pledged to help Batista."

"Can you imagine? I hear it's just handfuls of peasants in the mountains, and the troops are losing!"

A ding. Hit return.

"You know what that means. Batista will crack down. On *everybody*."

Nervous energy in the air. An uncertainty.

It's not that Dolores didn't want to see the President gone. But she had thought Daniel brash to run off to the mountains and feared every day that squads would come in the night, would shoot the whole family, dump their bodies in a hidden grave, burn their house, rape her girls. She feared Daniel joining the rebellion not because she disagreed with it in principle but because she had stopped believing any kind of change was possible. She wanted to live. And, even more important, wanted Carmen and Elena to live.

But life right now. Daniel brought home less some weeks than others, and they always lived on the precipice of hunger, of falling ill with no money for a doctor or a hospital. Daniel had to hand over half his already scanty earnings to some guy with Yanqui connections. And she knew the stories about the firing squads and the disappearances and the young girls who'd been whisked from their beds in the night because they caught the President's eye.

As stories of the military's defeats circled more and more,

Dolores began to see. She began to see, in whatever lay on the other side of the regime, something akin to her own do-over. If the rebels in the mountains succeeded, if her husband left and died a hero, if she woke up a new woman in a new country. She might dare to seek a future, any future, that wasn't *this*.

As it happened, Daniel did leave to the mountains after a skirmish with Batista's men depleted the ranks of guerrilleros and Fidel once more put out a call over Radio Rebelde. But before he did, Dolores came closer to death than she ever had before, even with her ribs broken, with her mouth pouring blood and her tooth in her hand, even closer than that.

Two months after Daniel killed a man for the first time, he looked for something, who knows what. He'd ducked under the bed and seen the curious slash in the mattress. And when he found the wad of money, when he dug his hand into the exposed spring coils and came out with a fistful of cash, he grabbed a sobbing Carmen and Elena by their hair, threw them into the bedroom they shared. Then he took Dolores by the neck as she washed dishes at the sink. He took her by the neck with one hand and with the other ripped off her dress and left her in her slip. He dragged her through the door.

He beat her as he usually did, except this time he did it right outside their house, where Dolores stood crouching and shivering, horrified that a neighbor might pass at any minute and witness her shame, her C-section-scarred belly and quivering thighs. When he was done pummeling her at the door, when he'd drawn a bloody gash across her cheek and punched her eye shut, he grabbed her by the hair and threw her back into the house, to the bedroom. Then he pulled his machete from behind the bed and held it over her.

She was aware, from movies and such, that some people saw their lives flash before them at the moment of death. But that didn't happen to her. She didn't see a montage: Dolores as a giggling child in her own mother's arms; Dolores wiggling up palm trees to knock down coconuts; Dolores afraid and exhilarated when a handsome man came looking for her; Dolores and a bloody, beautiful Carmen; Dolores nursing Elena as her mother lay dying. None of that happened.

Dolores didn't see. She felt: a roaring beast in her gut, salivating, frothing for another chance to open her mouth and form a word, any word. The beast found ferocity in her she'd never again recover. She apologized, of course. Sobbed and begged and pleaded and summoned her daughters' names in the hope of reaching the humanity in Daniel. But he swung. He swung and her hands sprang and she grabbed the handle with such strength, with such rage, that the machete halted inches from her face. Inexplicable. A Hollywood-worthy ending. She felt like Marilyn Monroe. A Cuban Marilyn Monroe in underwear with one eye swollen shut and smears of her own blood, who knew from where anymore, soaking her slip.

It was enough to stop Daniel: miracle. He crumbled to the floor, panting, then threw the machete across the room. "You fucking puta. You're lucky I didn't slit your throat."

She was Marilyn Monroe, and she had never felt more certain she could survive without Daniel.

And then Daniel left for the mountains again.

But this time, she listened to Radio Rebelde every day he was gone. She listened for any sign of defeat, that bombs would rain over the tropics. That Daniel would walk into a campo town thinking he'd meet sympathizers but then— gunshot to the face. That a snake the size of a palm trunk would slither into his tent, crush his neck in the night. Her money gone. He'd taken the cash from the mattress. But she didn't care. If she'd learned one thing from that beast in her, that beast that had absorbed death so she could live, it was this: She would survive. No matter what.

When news of Batista's defeat reached Dolores, she sat at her sewing machine, mending trousers for some wealthy city people, a job she'd secured via her underground typewriter-ladies circle. Circle of saviors. She wept before the silk dresses and pleated pants, waiting for Carmen to arrive home from school. Wept as Elena tugged at her hem and said, "Mamá café. Mamá café."

And then in the afternoon, to the city again. How the plaza came alive that day, rumblings and murmurings, singing peanut vendor, nannies with smiles on their faces patting little blond heads, Carmen and Elena making wishes over fountain coins that weren't theirs. Dead? Alive? Surely dead. For days, she waited for the postman with a letter announcing her widowhood or perhaps a compañero from the mountains with a beret in his hand over his heart . . . *I'm so sorry to inform you of this, comrade . . .*

Instead, Daniel showed again. Came through the door at dawn on a Wednesday before Dolores was up, when it was still dark outside. Walked right into their bedroom and kissed her atop the head.

"We won," he said to her. "Get up and get the cafetera going. Did you hear Fidel himself is coming to the city? Perhaps today, even."

She had no words. All Dolores could do as she lit the gas and placed the rusted metal contraption over the fire was think of the machete she'd purchased when Daniel left, tucked under the big guava bush behind their house. She'd sharpened it herself. She'd practiced the blow that could bring a fat sugarcane stalk thudding to the ground.

The girls ran to Daniel's side when they woke, hugged him tight, chattered away.

"Today we'll celebrate," Dolores said to them. "You can stay home from school, Carmen."

"Why?" Carmen looked up from her father's shoulder, where she'd burrowed her head.

"Things are going to be better now."

"What things?"

"All things, darling."

She needed a plan. The coffee bubbled, filled the kitchen with the heavy, burnt scent of dark roast. It rose like chimney smoke through the barrel, hot and fragrant. She poured three little cups. She needed Carmen bright awake in case they had to run at any minute. Dolores shaky, sticky, in the kitchen, bending over the stove. A shiver up her spine.

Little cups before Daniel and Carmen. She drank her own in a sip.

"Me too?" Carmen asked.

"Yes, cariño. Celebrate with a little cafecito."

She knew Daniel would never let her leave. He'd hunt her down; he'd find her. He'd said as much. She was most afraid for Carmen and Elena. If she left them. If she took them.

"What are you making?" Daniel slipped a cigar from the pocket of his shirt and lit it over the stove fire.

Dolores pushed open a window. "Tostadas. What else could I afford?" He ignored her remark. She cut slices of bread as Carmen peppered Daniel with questions.

"Why was work so many days?

"Where do you sleep or do you just work for days and days?

"How come you didn't even come home for lunch?

"What did you eat?"

"Café café café," Elena said, toddling on the ground.

"Both of you—quiet." Dolores slathered butter on a piece of bread. Outside, the chickens, causing commotion.

She would wait until night. Whatever she was going to do, she would have to do it at night. She toasted the bread on a pan, flattened it with a foil-wrapped brick, and pictured her own head crushed beneath that weight.

"I'm going out to look for a paper," Daniel said.

"But your bread?"

"When I get back, you can make me another one. I can't sit around. I'm too excited."

Relief. A few minutes to herself. Maybe even an hour if he stopped along the way to chat up neighbors and townspeople. The sun was out. The town would be buzzing.

As it was, Daniel took even longer. She paced and then cleaned to ward off her anxiety and then paced some more and then cleaned some more. She wondered what Daniel had felt when he killed a man for the first time and if it'd happened from afar, with a gun, or if he'd faced the man whose life he took, if Daniel had looked him in the eyes. And after? Did Daniel feel powerful? He'd decided a fate. That's all it was, killing a man, squeezing the time line a little. Who knew if that man Daniel had killed would have died anyway, struck by a car in a year or contracting an awful disease. Perhaps Daniel had spared him a worse fate.

Daniel left for three hours, and the whole time Dolores was sure Carmen and Elena wondered why their mother kept saying she loved them, why their mother wouldn't stop hugging them.

Dolores said they should celebrate. Daniel even gave her cash who knows from where to buy a whole pig from a neighbor, and they slaughtered it, made a hole in the ground, and left it to roast all day. The pig had screamed as Daniel slit its throat, and all Dolores could think was *Marilyn Monroe Marilyn Monroe.*

She got him drunk. Glass of rum after glass of rum. Some with Coca-Cola, bright and popping in the glass. Some pure, dark rum with an ice cube, frothy fire down the throat. She feared he'd grow angry as he drank more; it happened enough. But he was too elated from the victory that few even knew about yet, unless they were also glued to the radio. Jolly and red faced into the evening, swinging the girls in circles and promising them dolls and gifts.

Carmen and Elena delighted as well. Their mother doting on them, unable to let go; their father merry and generous, offering the world.

"Daddy, I love you!" Carmen shouted as Daniel hoisted her in the air and Beny Moré's trombone shrieked.

"I love you, mi linda!" Daniel spun her and spun her.

Dolores made her move after she put the girls to bed. They'd complained, of course, asked to keep the party going. Carmen most of all. But Dolores told the girls they'd get their promised dollhouse if only they said their prayers and shut their eyes. Then Dolores dressed in her most formfitting wiggle dress and dabbed perfume on her neck. She painted her lips red.

Daniel at the table with another glass of Cuba Libre before him, already piss-drunk, slurring the words to "Dolor y Perdón" with his head down. *Yo no supe comprender tu cariño, / vida mía, cariñito.*

Fulgencio Batista was in the Dominican Republic, where he had fled in a plane in the night with over $700 million in cash and fine art. As Dolores waltzed toward Daniel, President Rafael Trujillo was welcoming the fellow dictator into his palace, probably consoling him. Perhaps they, too, shared a bottle of rum. And Dolores was guiding Daniel by the hand and he was wobbling and slurring. She was laying him on the couch.

"You look so good, mami," he slurred. Daniel held an arm toward Dolores and brought her down on top of him. He kissed her neck. She sighed and moaned. She had planned to do whatever it took, to bear it, to hope Daniel had sex with her and then immediately fell asleep, as he so often did. But she didn't have to go that far. He kissed her neck, and then turned his head, eyes fluttering, and drifted into easy, drunken sleep. He started to snore.

Dolores waited a few minutes to be sure he wasn't going to wake. Then she eased away from Daniel's body and gently kicked off her high heels. Barefoot, she tiptoed out the back door and shut it behind her. She had to feel her way through the dirt and shrubs in near perfect darkness. In the middle of July, even the nights were made of an engulfing, wet heat. She could feel herself damp under the tight linen of her red dress and could feel the spongey dirt give way beneath her. She found the machete. Hesitated only a moment before grabbing its handle.

Funny how the mind protects us. Dolores can remember nothing of what happened after that and has only imagined scenarios. She must have tiptoed back into the house. She must have shut the door behind her. How did she creep up to Daniel as he snored? Was she behind the sofa or before him? She must have stabbed him dozens of times, there was so much blood. So much blood could only have come from slash after slash into Daniel's chest and stomach, slash after slash after slash.

What she does remember: Daniel waking at some point and screaming. How she feared the girls would hear and wake or a neighbor in the distance would catch hold of the desperate shouts and come running, phone the police. (Were there police? Who was in charge, now that the rebels had defeated Batista?) But Daniel had been unable to stop Dolores in his drunken stupor; his screams had quieted quickly. All that was left then was Dolores breathing hard with a blood-streaked machete in her hand, was Daniel still as the moon, covered in sticky wounds, and soaking red deep into the couch.

Dolores waited even later—it must have been two in the morning. And panting and sweating and heaving, she pushed that whole couch out the back door and into the little plot behind the house. Few people could see into the back of Dolores and Daniel's home. The nearest neighbor was a mile away, and she couldn't make out the house past the thick bushes and palm trees. She took the coals they'd used to roast the pig and spread the same gasoline over their stony surface. She assembled wooden planks she'd saved to make a pit. She lit that whole couch and her unmoving husband on fire and watched them blaze into the sky, into the night. She watched the flames pop and crackle like a million gathered fireflies. There were no stars that she could see, but the flames were enough. As if a moon had descended into her own backyard. She could hardly believe what she had done.

Not until morning, when all that was left was a pile of ash and Dolores looked down at her body covered in blood and soot and sweat and could have jumped into the fire herself. But what of Carmen and Elena then? She'd done what needed to be done. She'd had no choice. She would spread the word—of her hero husband, a martyr who died bravely in the mountains. When people would claim they'd seen him, she'd question their dates, play the confused grieving wife. She'd tell the girls their father had left again, one final battle; it wasn't victory yet like he'd said. She'd stand at the road as the parade heralded Fidel Castro through the streets in a couple of days and she would weep, she would laugh and weep and wave, she would hold her girls in the air and tell them the time for crying was over. She would dance.

How was she to know that Carmen had stood at the back door that night? That she'd seen her father's face slowly consumed by licking flames and tiptoed back into the house? In fifteen years, Carmen would board a plane to Miami, and Dolores would never see her again. She would think it was politics that had divided her from her firstborn daughter.

11

OTHER GIRL

Jeanette
Miami, 2006

The first time I see the woman, she is buying cold cream. What she wants, she says, is a moisturizer that doesn't feel heavy, doesn't sit on her skin like so much weight. I lay out her options: whipped argan oil, cold-pressed and refined; our new microbeading exfoliating lotion with gentle 7 percent alpha hydroxy; the bestselling hyaluronic-acid-plus-B-vitamins gel with all-day-stay technology, patent pending. Her red fingernails tap the counter as she slides a credit card with her other hand. She buys all of them.

I can't take my eyes off her. She reminds me of my mother. I think this is what draws me to her, what makes it so I can't take my eyes off her. I haven't seen her, my mother, in a month. I have only one day off from the store each week, and I have to choose: spend my day off with her or with Mario. My mother doesn't know about Mario. She only knows I have a job again. I haven't lost it again.

The woman reminds me of my mother because she looks breakable. But also immaculate. Breakable and immaculate. I see her almost every single week, and she always shops during the day, like so many other women. She wears red-soled heels, carries snakeskin bags. Looks like she smells of Chanel No. 5—no, something even more expensive, that Jean Patou thousand-dollar bottle with ambergris from sperm whales and eight thousand jasmine flowers. I make ten dollars an hour, but the lexicon of wealth still roots in me. I can't scrub my childhood off. *You're simply and unobtrusively classy, like a Celine bag,* I say to her in a daydream.

The same day she buys cream from me, the woman tells me her name. I say Isabel is a beautiful name. I get the feeling that she doesn't want to leave the counter; she lingers. Her skin is so bright and taut that it glistens. It is the skin of expensive facials, chemical peels. Things I do not seek at nineteen. You have beautiful skin, I say, because I do not know what else to say. My mother has the same skin, and I see her leaning into the mirror sometimes, running a finger over each cheek, examining her pores. She is fond of telling me that she, too, used to have skin like mine. That I ought to stay out of the sun. As if the sun is my problem. As if my problems don't flourish under the glare of artificial light.

The other reason I haven't seen my mother in a month is that I refuse to see my mother in her own home—once my own home—as long as my father is there. She doesn't understand. He's sick and I should see him, she says. He can't even drink anymore, she says. But I don't go home and she doesn't come to my new home and so we always meet in some café or Cuban restaurant—and on most of my days off, I don't want to go. So she just calls and says, Are you okay? And I say, I'm okay. And she says, Can I go see you? And I say I'm busy and she sighs a lot and then there is just so much silence on the phone that we hang up because neither of us can handle so much silence.

The same day of the face cream and the woman-like-my-mother, Mario nods off on the kitchen table, where he racks up a line and I eat dinner by myself because he isn't hungry all night.

He has a new job: dispensary tech at a pain clinic. He's been there a month, and for a month he's been slipping Oxy pill by pill in his socks. Easier than anyone would think, he says. He sells them. He wants me to quit my job at the department store. He wants to take care of me, he says.

I've *never* needed the job, I tell him. I'm not at the department store for the money. My parents pay the rent. They give me money for almost anything we want. I work behind a counter in a department store that overwhelms me with perfume and glittering floor tiles because I don't know what else to do and I ruined my chances at college exactly as my parents said I would ruin my chances at college. Because if I sit at home, I want to disappear.

At night, I flip through the channels from bed. I click back to a *Law & Order* rerun because, oh my God, it's the woman, the woman from the store—but it's not her at all. It's just a brunette who on closer scrutiny does not look like the woman and does not even look like my mother. *Criminal Intent, Trial by Jury.*

I call my mother anyways. I believe in signs. We make plans to meet at La Palma the coming weekend, and she asks if I want to say hello to my father and I say hell no as usual.

Mario is completely knocked out next to me and I wrap my arm around his head and cradle it as I talk to him. I think about if his head were a baby and run my nails over his cheek. He looks so helpless this way. I just want to protect this head baby. From what, I don't know.

It's been only a month, together, in my apartment. And I

want him to stay so bad that I am afraid. No man has ever given me so much attention, made me feel like some kind of savior. I am constantly calibrating who to be, what kind of woman Mario wants, though I know that he likes me because he thinks me the kind of woman not constantly calibrating who to be. For him.

So I try to be all things and nothing, and sometimes I feel that I am dissolving and I lean into the mirror, like my mother, and touch my face: I am still here. It bothers me that I can never really see myself as someone else can, as Mario can. I have to trust that the reflection is right. I have to trust that seeing in reverse is close enough to seeing straight on.

Mario likes that I'm willing to try it all, that I'm willing to go there, that I am not a barrier to whatever he wants. You're not like other girls, he says, and I wind the words tight around me, a cape. The world is full of other girls—shiny-haired, giggle-glowing, simultaneously pure and sex-enthralled, groups of them, worlds of them, walking in community, writhing under club lights, running through parks. But if he says he doesn't like other girls, if I am not an "other girl," he will be mine, not theirs.

Except that I know deep down that I *am* other girls. They spin in me and around me. I am of them: my coworker who has been wearing the same lipstick shade, Barely Legal, every day since some guy leaned over the counter and complimented her on the color. My mother who buys and buys, sure she hasn't found the right cream the right needle the right dress to win a man back, so she keeps trying. She keeps buying. Sasha who is no longer my best friend, because her boyfriend told her he thought she should dress more like me (clarified: more sexy) and so she realized I was not an other girl to him or that she was not a special girl, a chosen girl, or that all the categories collapse at the behest of the men who make them and that it is just easier to pretend that we have any control in the first place. Control is pushing me away.

Mario has no idea. He has no idea the time and energy I spend trying to hide all this from him. Instead of telling him, I tell myself: Do it all. Never say no. No is for other girls.

I met Mario in rehab, my first one. I wasn't really addicted, I still don't think, even though yeah, yeah, I know. It was just coke and it wasn't even every day but I'd lost my office job when I failed a drug test and my mother was relentless and finally I said okay, I can afford to check out for twenty-eight days if it will get you off my back. It was a religious place, twelve steps, all that. The staff didn't really care. They were making money. I never talked.

Almost everyone made me sad except Mario. Abstinence only, which meant that Mario, who was there trying to wean off a Lortab habit, couldn't get any medication assistance. So of course rehab failed. Of course he left rehab with a new dealer contact (his roommate) and a job at the clinic (also via his roommate, former employee). It was okay, though. Mario doesn't believe in that abstinence-only bullshit, and unless you've used opioids, you wouldn't understand, he says. Like addiction is more like a spectrum. It's more like a balance. Like if you're strung out and your whole life is fucked up, then yeah, you need to stop. But if you're mostly clean and you want to indulge in *something* once in a while . . . how realistic is it that you'll never use any kind of substance ever again?

He got kicked out of a sober-living house when they found his Percs, and by then we were talking every day and I said, Come, I'll take care of you. Mario believes in gray areas, and people like my mom believe everything is black and white, and I'm not sure where I fall, except that Mario is the smartest man I've ever known. He can explain everything like how buying a house is the smartest investment and we can get a mortgage even without our parents' help and even if we don't have our own money and he never asks me about my family and he clings to me like I am the piece he's been missing all this time.

I learn so much from Mario and I start to wonder if this is what I missed not going to college like him. I listen and it feels like growth. I listen and sometimes I drink and sometimes I do a little coke and stay up all night talking or molly and fuck and fuck or benzos when I need to finally get some sleep. And it's fine. It's mostly the weekends. And Mario, he doesn't even touch the Oxys, just sells them or trades them for Percs but it's just to keep the migraines at bay, not even as much as before. I'm afraid of addiction, I've seen what it did to my father. So we're careful. I don't say no—I'm not another girl—but I'm careful. I hug his head.

———

The woman's husband comes around Christmastime. The woman's husband is handsome, with legs too spindly for his body, like a gazelle in a suit. Isabel walks him to my counter and says, he needs a cream for his dry skin but nothing that smells too flowery. Then she walks away to browse shoes, and I tell the husband about our line of men's products in blue-black containers that suggest sailorly conquest and rapacious strength. I'm sorry for my wife, the husband says, she sounds so dumb sometimes. I don't know how to respond, so I say do you use a daily antioxidant to battle signs of premature aging? He frowns and walks away. I place a hand on the cold glass counter and picture it cracking under my weight. I am thin and wispy like a bowl of feathers, like crumpled paper tumbling in the wind. Nothing cracks in my presence.

—·—

At home, Mario nods off again. All he does lately is sleep. I make dinner and set the table, but he does not wake. I curl beside him on the couch and say hello, I am home, but he does not wake. I lay my head over his chest and listen to his heartbeat and I kiss his chin. Love me, I whisper. Look how happy we are, I say.

—·—

I don't understand why you don't at least come home, my mother says. I mean, just to visit. I'm not saying you need to live there.

We are sitting in her car and it's pouring rain outside, the kind so dissipated it almost looks like it's raining in reverse. She is dropping me off at the mall after taking me to get a haircut. She is wary now of giving me big chunks of cash but wants me to do my hair at her fancy place anyway.

A woman needs to have *presencia,* she says, and then she starts going into her thing about how she always puts on a full face of makeup every morning even if she's just staying home and doing nothing, which I will never understand.

Mom, I say. You should leave him.

Who, your dad? she says, laughing. She is staring straight ahead at the water hitting the windshield like how she sounds typing with her long, perfectly round nails.

Do you realize he just lies in bed all the time now? she says. Do you realize how sick he is? I mean, *I'm* the one who has the power now. The seats in her car are heated, which seems like such a waste in Miami, but I'm comforted none-theless, tucked into the nest-like embrace of warm leather. I try to make myself smaller, shrink deeper.

But you fight all the time, I say, and I lean my head against the passenger-side window. I watch another mall employee, plastic bag held over her head, running toward the door of the department store. I am glad to be early. I am glad not to have to run in the rain.

My mother pinches the top of her nose like she's getting a headache. It's the kind of thing she does when she's being dramatic. I love her, I really do—I just wish she made better choices.

Jeanette.

What?

You're being ridiculous. We don't even fight anymore. He doesn't even have the energy if he wanted to.

She places a hand between my shoulder blades, a thing she does when she wants me to stop slouching.

And anyway, that was the alcohol, you know that, she says. That was a disease, a disorder. He did things and said things he would not have done or said if he wasn't sick. You should understand that.

I slouch again as soon as she moves her hand away.

When we used to fight, you know when he used to drink . . . I have accepted that was not the man I married, she says, and that's not the man he is now. He's just an old man. I just want us to be, oh, a normal family again.

Now it is my turn to laugh. Mom, I say. I'm nineteen. It's a bit too late for that, don't you think? And he's not drinking, because he can't. And it is the man he was. And I don't love him, okay? I've decided I don't love him.

My voice snags in my throat and comes out hoarse, and then before I know it I'm gulping and crying and she's looking at me and shaking her head like she just doesn't understand and I'm thinking, say it, say it, and still I can't.

Just choose me or him! I scream at her instead.

But I would always choose you! she yells back at me, and now she looks like she's going to cry too. I just don't understand why you think I need to make that choice! Why we both can't be happy and healthy. I just don't get why you don't want me to be happy. You think you're protecting me? You think I want you to hate your father?

And she's rambling again about how he's better now and they don't fight anymore and none of it is about me, so I start to gather my bag at my feet and wipe my eyes, glad it will look like rain smeared my eyeliner.

Wait, she says, leaning over the console between us. She puts her arms around me and pulls me toward her and I end up just leaning my head on her chest while she strokes my hair like when I was small. Outside the rain lets up. A valet in front of the department store starts to wander over to us, but he sees us and awkwardly stops and goes back to his station, glancing over every few minutes. I look up at my mom, and she looks tired.

You know I would do anything for you, right? she says, leaning her head back. I just want to see you well, she says.

I know, Mommy, I say. I know.

I'm late to work that day, but I don't even care.

———·———

And that day the woman comes back with her husband. He holds her bicep as he walks her over to my counter, his knuckles red but not cracked like Mario's, and I think, I know his hands would be soft in mine. I think, hers would be too.

I thought you bought a moisturizer last week, the woman says to the husband. She fiddles with the sapphire ring on her finger. I thought last week I brought you—

We didn't come here last week, honey, the man interrupts.

No, we did—I mean I think we did—and I said you didn't want anything flowery, the woman says.

Honey, the man says, the fact that you keep imagining these things is really starting to worry me.

He smiles at me, and the smile is so warm I imagine a stone that sloughs the dead skin from my body, sloughs away the rain, the car, my mother's hand on my back, Mario sleeping more and more and more.

I am so sorry, the man says to me, and I want his hand gripping my biceps too. When he buys the cream, he does what no one has ever done for me—hands me a tip, fifty dollars. You're beautiful, he says, and his wife looks away.

———

I agree to see her again. She bombards me with phone calls, and what can I do? I say okay, okay, fine, and I pop some Xanax so that I can at least relax but it just makes me sleepy.

My mother orders a disco volador with guava and cheese and I order a greasy pile of churros that I dip into hot chocolate so thick it's more like sweet mud. We sit outside on uncomfortable metal seats like playground benches under the multicolored tarp that reminds me of one of those circus-looking termite tents that engulf the unluckiest homes in Miami. The traffic on Calle Ocho zooms by, headlights blink and circle, neon signs light up the night. Another pain clinic across the street. Another dark window. I've accompanied Mario to his clinic a couple of times to pick up his paychecks. I notice them everywhere now.

They have blossomed like someone scattered seeds from above and hit every strip mall, every billboard, every back page of the free weekly. There are discounts and two-for-ones, promises of no wait time and in-and-out appointments, cash only, three hundred, twenty-four hours, doctors on call.

Walk-ins welcome, HGH and testosterone, too, discount with MRI, commissions on every customer referred, black-out windows, flashing OPEN sign. The massage parlor next door. Check cashing across the street.

Mario tells me some of the doctors don't even bother with pretense, just ask, What do you want? How much? The pharmacies on-site behind bulletproof glass. The clinic managers who carry heat. The parking lots crawling with out-of-state license plates: Kentucky, Virginia, Maine. The Oxy highway, the Oxy Express. The patients, all tapping feet and abscess scars, lining up outside the doors some days, some already sniffling and rheumy, itching—no, *dying*—to stave off the sickness. The doctors barely glancing their way, the doctors with their fat gold watches. So unlike my father the doctor, my father the classy super-clean. The money is *fucking insane*, Mario says. I just have to get a bigger piece of the pie, he says.

My mother cuts her sandwich with a knife and fork. She looks so out of place among the greasy discarded trays and the line of men in undershirts, women in stretch pants, the cafecito-to-go attendants in their starched white shirts and hairnets.

My mother chews and swallows. She runs her tongue over her teeth, a habit when she's nervous. One I can't stand. Her lips are my own lips, naturally plump, slightly crooked when she smiles. We've been told, always, our smiles look fake. But even doubled over in genuine laughter, that crooked smile.

How are you? she says. Veins on her hands. I wonder if mine will look like that. If I will notice as they change or if I will just wake up one day, wondering when green lattice emerged from under my skin.

I want to cry again and I don't even know why. I want to tell my mother to take me home. I want, again, to tell her about my father, but I won't even tell myself about my father. I think about this often, about whether the past is real if we don't bring it into the present. Tree falling in the forest and all that.

I'm okay, I say.

I don't know if I am the tree or the no one who doesn't hear it.

My mother searches my eyes. Runs her tongue over her teeth.

See me, I think. *Just this once, see me, Mommy.*

My mother opens her mouth like she's going to say something, closes it again. Finally she speaks. Your skin looks so good, my mother says, and there is sadness on her face, I can see it. But I just feel so much relief.

———·———

Mario was supposed to get a Lortab script but the doctor wasn't in and the other doctor was too busy. I should have jacked a script pad, he says. Bro, my boy at the clinic fucking sells them. He's in such a bad mood. Calm down baby, I say. I offer him some of my coke, but he's like nah, I'm already too on edge. You know what, he says, let's see what all the hillbilly hype is about. He's been avoiding the Oxy because (1) it's stronger and more pure, and he isn't trying to get super-hooked or anything, and (2) that's where the money is and everyone knows that once you dip in your own supply, you're screwing up. It's cheaper here in Florida, but Mario's been talking to his friend and they are planning the drive up to Virginia, see if they can set up something steady.

Fuck it, he says. It's one time.

I give him my fifty-dollar tip. It's like I paid for it, I say.

We hold each other that night and I want to simultaneously die, laugh.

The fan whirs above us and I watch a mosquito perched on the edge of a blade. How can it stay so still when everything is spinning? I wonder, but I wake up with bites all over my body.

——·——

My mother invites me to Versailles for the Sunday tamal en cazuela special. It's our third weekend seeing each other in a row, it's hard to believe. She knows tamal en cazuela is my favorite. I don't like Versailles, its combination of "yellow rice with beans, please" tourist crowd and old guard prim-and-proper Cuban Americans. But the tamal en cazuela. I live for the salty mush—corn, lard, pork—burning my tongue. We end the meal with cortaditos, and my mother places a hand on mine. She is so uncomfortable showing emotion but then she cracks, and the crack then breaks me and I rush to put up the façade again. We do this dance over and over and over again, and it feels worse than not talking at all.

I know I have failed you in some way, she says. And I just wish I knew how. I just wish I knew how to fix whatever is broken between us.

I can't look up. I can't look up from my coffee, from the foam dissolving into the tiny cup. Tell her, I think, tell her.

But what would it do other than widen the gulf? We are already two continents; impossible to imagine a bridge could even exist. I wish to dissolve into my cup, I wish to dissolve on the tongue, to be sugar and not this bitter, watery substance in the shape of Girl.

It is easier to go further back, to deflect past with past. I ask about Cuba again.

My mother sighs.

There is nothing to say, she says. But I'll tell you this: I was not rich like the other Cubans who came at that time.

It is more than she has ever said.

So how did you survive? I say, and what I really mean is how will I walk out of these gaudy gold-etched doors into the wet open mouth of a hot Miami afternoon and survive, and then the day after that, how will I survive, and then the day after that, how will I survive, and when will I stop feeling exhausted from all the surviving?

My mother laughs. Your father, she says. That's how. Do you understand now why it's been so hard for me to say no to that man all our life together?

See me, see me, I think. *Just for this one moment, see me. I am sinking, I am screaming, Tell me how to live, Mommy.*

I dip a finger into my cup, and she watches, perplexed, as I place it in my mouth.

I want to go, I say. To Cuba.

My mother laughs sarcastically. She rolls her eyes. It's so good, my mother says. It's so good to see you doing well. I mean, I think you are well. Are you well?

I nod. I can feel the sugar crystals dissolving on my tongue. Everything sweet. I run my tongue over my teeth.

The woman still comes alone during the week. But now I notice what I hadn't noticed before. Her eyes are red-rimmed like my father's last time I saw him, months and months ago. Cirrhosis had made him all blood vessel, bloat. But the woman is not all blood vessel or bloat, though her hands tremble each time she picks up a shoe to inspect it.

I watch her from my counter right across from the shoes. She always makes it a point to come to my counter even when she doesn't buy something. But she is forgetful and often buys the same product she bought a day before or returns

something she already has. She apologizes so often I begin to
call her Mrs. Sorry to myself.

I see the woman during the holiday season, after Mario
loses his job. I see her the week one of the clinic doctors
catches Mario slipping pills into his shoe. He paces the whole
week, yelling and throwing things. He knows he won't be
arrested, because the authorities are already starting to crack
down on some of the clinics, inspectors and whatnot, all political he says, which means nothing to me but to him means
he won't be arrested because the clinic won't call the cops.

But still. He'll become a patient now, he'll need to pay
for the bottles and doctor shop, just like everybody else.
The profit margin smaller. I ask my mother for a little more
money so we can invest it, and she asks for what and I say
I need new clothes, for work. And I tell Mario I am getting
money from my mother, thinking that will make him feel
better, one less problem, one way I make things better, and
it does a little.

He hugs me and tells me I am the best thing to ever happen to him and it's so hard for me to let go of that warm
cologne embrace, needing this, wanting this so bad.

But the woman: she is back with her husband and they
browse the shoes and she does not come to my counter. She
just passes by and we make eye contact. We both smile at the
same time.

———┆———

I don't know when the twenties become forties. I barely notice when the forties become eighties. I do remember my
first. Pale pink in my hand, like a tutu, like the one I wore to
my dance recital in second grade. Or like the houses in my
subdivision, or guava juice from a can, or dusk when the sky

eats the sun and traffic stalls and I don't make it home until pink turns to red, red turns to black.

The first: Mario put the pill in his mouth and the coating turned to jelly. He rubbed it off on his white shirt. Forever we'd be walking around with streaks of Easter-pale on our shirts, baby pink, orange, green. There is something so childlike about this life, ours.

Mario toyed with the pill. He shaved it down—took a hose clamp he'd stolen from an auto store, used it like a cheese grater. The Oxy turned to dust. Mario racked up a line. I knew how to sniff—not that different from the coke, I figured—but this was different, different texture, different taste in the back of my throat. Mario told me not to tilt my head back. And then: I turned to dust. I turned to sitting by the ocean wrapped in towels or sinking into cotton candy clouds, or warm rain washing clean, or holding Mario's hand, soft and slippery, maybe velvet, maybe maple syrup. No, a guest bathroom. Let me explain.

A memory: Hurricane Andrew, 1992. We crouched into the only room with no windows, the hallway guest bathroom. I don't think I'd ever been confined in a space so small with my parents. This was before my father's drinking had gotten as bad as it did, before my mother had lost layers of herself until she was emotionally weightless, onionskin.

Back then there was something like TV love still. Back then there was me, small and shaking each time I heard a crash, a Category 5 wind whip to crush a car beneath a palm, to blow a roof into the night, send a balcony rail sailing. But I wasn't afraid. Mom smelled like soap, like clean. A candle flickered on the bathroom sink; we'd lost power already. She wore a black nightgown with red flowers, and I thought her the very definition of beauty, womanhood, future me, the person emulated in every game of dress-up.

Dad stoic, patting me on the back. I was so used to seeing him in scrubs or a suit, and plaid pajama pants felt like a sign I'd crossed into a more intimate space, that we'd be a closer family that night. The bathtub was stopped up and filled with water that sparkled in the candlelight. I could see us reflected when I looked up at the bathroom mirror, and I wondered what others saw when they looked at my family. We looked close.

At one point the wind picked up outside and we heard the loud snap of a branch and my parents both hugged me, together. Heroin would take me there. Heroin would be the only time traveler I'd meet in this life. So safe in that warm bubble, that eye of the storm. Everything raging outside, and me, warm and embraced. What does it say about a person when she doesn't want one of the deadliest hurricanes in Florida history to end?

———•———

But I'll never recover that first time. Or that bathroom. I'll rack up lines and swear I'll never mainline, trying to recover that first high. Then buy rigs pretending I'm a diabetes patient needing insulin. Skin-pop, needle into the skin but not hitting a vein, not yet. Share a rig with Mario. I'll run out of money and the clinics will shutter and the country will catch on and my mother will catch on and the pills will dry up completely so Mario will buy from his boy for way cheaper for that first high. I'll even knowingly buy pandas or heroin stepped on with fentanyl because anything anything anything. To recover that first high. Nobody telling me it will never come. Nobody telling me life will be a daily quest to stave off the sickness and I won't even feel good anymore. Dope made us sick, then it healed us. Don't believe anyone who tells you dope isn't love.

But there is no heroin yet. There is no Operation Shut Down Every Pill Mill. We are far from the dollar-a-milligram to come. We are far from treatment bed after treatment bed after treatment bed, half of them scams, but I don't know this yet. We are far from my mother screaming she'd lose her life to save mine, she'd lose her life to hear me say I want to live. Mario and me: we are headed to hell hand in hand, but I don't know this yet. I just know it's not one Oxy anymore. I just know I'm falling in love too. With it. With him. Becoming the same thing. Falling in love. Falling in love.

Nobody says rising in love.

And the husband with his wife standing before me and the husband says, she doesn't want to get an eye lift even though I tell her she looks like shit with all those wrinkles. He tells me I'm pretty again and says, give her something that will at least make it better. I lay out the options on the counter, and the woman looks from one bottle to the next and I notice her eyes begin to water and I beg her in my head please don't cry please don't cry please don't cry. She doesn't cry.

I thought I came here, she says instead, her voice shaking. I thought I—

She doesn't want to get an eye lift even though I tell her she looks like shit, the husband says.

My hand is shaking and her hand is shaking and all I can think is a needle doesn't really hurt that much, it's just a pinch.

When the woman walks away, the husband hands me a blue-black container in its package and says also, he would like to return this.

I say, you didn't buy that here. We don't sell that here.

Yes, you do, he says, I see it right behind you on that shelf. I have the receipt, he says.

You didn't buy that here, I repeat.

And I know I'll be fired and I know that neither Mario nor I will have a job and I know that he will never love me like I need him to love me, which is to say a love that erases everything that came before, and I know that he will end me but I feel like a truck, I feel like a bag bursting with rocks, I feel like I could crush everything beneath my weight.

You didn't buy that here, I say. I will not accept this, I say.

12

MORE THAN WE THINK

Ana
Mexico, 2019

She was only thirteen, but Ana was not afraid of death. She'd already seen it up close—how death had devoured her mother bit by bit, from the inside out, until what remained became apparent: a husk, a whisper, something you could mourn alive, not her mother at all. So she faced the river brave. She watched its muddy current swallow vines and leaves. She felt its power beneath her feet, how the placid shore hid a deeper hunger ahead.

The pollero handed her a black garbage bag in which to place her few possessions—a tattered backpack that contained a ziplock with all her important documents and a cell phone with an American SIM card she'd purchased from a gas station. She stripped to her underwear beside the dozen others who did the same—a few children and teens like her, mostly, and four adult women, two men. She stuffed her clothes, a yellowed Hello Kitty shirt and dirt-streaked jeans, into the bag. She tied a double knot.

A little girl beside her began to whimper.

Her older brother, a teenager, placed a hand over her mouth.

"Shut up before he hears you," he whispered as the girl placed a hand over his. She stopped crying.

The pollero had guided them to a large black van by the shore hidden in the scrub. Now he opened the back doors to several tires secured with rope. He held a flashlight in his teeth as he motioned to the group. He wanted them to drag a tire each, to help the little kids. He'd gone over it earlier.

Ana rubbed her legs together for warmth. All around her, thick brush scratched her ankles and mud coated her shoes. She trudged behind the others and pulled at a tire that bounced once on the ground and fell on its side. She struggled to lift the tire from the sludge and roll it toward the river. Some of the smallest kids shared a float with a sibling or adult, pushing alongside them, too little to really help. The adults instructed them, watched over them.

The pollero showed the group how to position themselves onto the tire so their upper body was supported. Ana squinted. She could barely make out his features in the dark, the cave of his black eyes and the long, thick hair he wore in a ponytail. He had on a hooded sweatshirt and dark corduroy pants that concealed the gun she knew he carried.

He'd shown it to them back in Monterrey, as they huddled in a one-room stash house before the next leg of the trip. He'd shown it while instructing them not to speak, to listen to every instruction, the code word should anyone pull them off a bus. The kids had stared wide-eyed. The adults had barely batted an eye.

Ana was the only one who started the trip already in Mexico. The others had journeyed for a month or more, from El Salvador, Guatemala, Honduras. They spoke little to one another. Their accents were noticeable; you never knew whom to trust. And a couple of them spoke Mam, K'iche', barely any Spanish at all. Ana couldn't remember quieting for so long. Other than a few whispered words—*Where's the bathroom? I think one of the children is sick*—Ana hadn't spoken in weeks.

The pollero instructed them on how to dog-paddle once they hit the water, even through the waist-high parts of the river, as he waited for a call from a lookout. The mud could swallow them like quicksand if they touched the ground, he said. They would drown and no one would be able to help them if the Border Patrol didn't come. They needed to paddle with their feet and hold their bags on their heads or with their teeth. Most of the people in the group hoped Border Patrol would catch them. Hoped they could start their asylum process on the other side and not in a tent camp. But the pollero had instructed some of the adults and older teens on where to go to try to blend in if they weren't caught. What streets to look for, what houses.

But right now, all Ana could see was water. Water like polished black stone. Ana could make out more bushes, more dirt, on the other side. The sides looked the same. Everything scrub, dirt, her own shivering body. During the day in Miguel Alemán, the sun was brutal and unrelenting. She'd folded her one clean shirt under a baseball cap just to protect her neck from sunburn. It was already peeled and raw, because they'd spent the day camped out and hiding at another part of the river.

They'd waited to cross but there were too many patrols on the other side. At that part of the river, there'd been no hint of breeze or even life. Just brush, tumbleweed, straw-colored dust that she'd expelled into tissue. She'd breathed so much sand she pictured it coating her lungs, its own desert beside her heart, a dune under her ribs.

But tonight was opposite, dry ice. It hurt to breathe. The

mud was cold. She knew the water would be too. She knew the cold would wipe the fear, and she wanted to be there already, in the water, floating on her back, though she knew that wouldn't be the case.

"I don't want to go in," the little girl in pigtails whispered beside her, teary.

"You have to," Ana told her. "It's going to be okay."

"My mom is on the other side," she said.

"We're going to be okay."

The girl reminded Ana of herself, of the trunk of a car, the cold of metal, of hospital machines. Of when she'd been motherless for days after her mother's detention, taken in by a stranger and wondering if she'd ever see her own family again.

The pollero got the call. Border Patrol agents switched shifts and would leave their patrol cars empty with the headlights on. A one-hour window, what they'd waited for all day. He whispered directions, thrust their tires.

Motherless, motherless again.

The adults pushed the kids forward as best they could. A few sniffled and whimpered; one yelped when her feet touched the water. Ana gripped her plastic bag with one hand and dragged the tire with the other. Her feet touched the icy water, and the mud became thicker, more greedily sucking. She lifted each foot with effort and finally gave up and slid through the muck.

The water was thicker than she had imagined. She'd pictured a swift river and currents she'd have to battle with all her might. But the river was rather narrow, and the water swampy, muddy. Ana could barely see before her, but she was guided by the shapes on the other side. She plodded until the water drenched her waist, and she remembered the pollero had told them to swim. She waded with one hand holding the bag on her head and the other grasping the tire. All around her, the others did the same, quiet, the only sound water splashing. Ana tried to wipe her eyes with her forearm but streaked mud across her face. Her eyes stung. She had only waded for minutes but already her arms felt tired, her shoulder muscles burned. She kicked and kicked but was making it across at a crawling pace. Maybe there *was* a current.

Ana heard a yelp and the commotion of splashing water.

Behind her, the pigtailed girl who had gone in with her was thrashing and crying out. "I'm stuck! I'm stuck!" she wailed.

Her brother, holding himself afloat beside her, leaned over his tire and pulled at her arms. Water lapped over the little girl in spurts. Her head bobbed in and out of the water.

Ana froze, unsure whether to turn back and swim the feet that separated her from the girl. But one of the older women, closer, made it to the girl and pulled at her from the other side.

"My feet!" the girl cried. "The river is eating me!" She splashed and wailed each time her head went under.

"Quiet!" the older woman whispered loudly. "Stop yelling!"

Others along the ant trail of tire and body stopped and looked over. But slowly, as if an escalator had restarted, the bodies moved forward again. Standing still meant the current pushed the group further askew of the bushes for which they aimed. Ana began to kick again too. She reasoned there was no use in dooming herself if another was helping the girl. But there was an ugly calculation in her decision too— she also reasoned that there was no use if the girl couldn't be helped. She tasted her own tears, or maybe sweat, her own salt. The sound of legs paddling and splashing. The pigtailed girl quieting. The whole night too quiet. *She'll be okay.* Snaking her way forward. She could make out the shore, could see a bank and the patchy grass that framed it. Soon she would touch ground in the country that made her, expelled her. But Roma, Texas, meant nothing to her. Would Miami? Miami without her mother. She was crying again.

Ana was so young when she had first traveled to the United States. She could no longer make out the real memories from those instilled by her mother's stories. Could no longer tell what had actually shaped her from what she'd been told had shaped her, should've shaped her. Somebody else's story. She could close her eyes and see the trunk of the car, musty and hot, pinpricks for light and air over a piece of cardboard that covered her.

Of her actual life in the US, though, she remembered more. She'd lived first in an apartment somewhere else in Texas with three other migrant families, sharing a twin bed with her mother. Then a friend had told her mother about a job working for a housekeeping company in Miami. So they had traveled by bus, Ana splayed on her mother's legs so they'd only have to purchase one ticket.

They had lived in Miami five years, first in a small, roach-filled apartment in Homestead and then in a town house in the Kendall suburbs. The last had been the happiest years of her life that she could remember—an elementary school she loved with a huge jungle gym under the sun, weekends playing in the ball pit of a McDonald's across the street from their complex, trips to the beach, barbecues at the park. She'd had no idea how tenuous a life she'd borrowed.

Then her mother taken. Arriving home from school to a locked door, an empty house. A neighbor—Janet? J-something?—took her in for a few days before officers came for Ana too. Then family detention, a jail for mothers, babies. A transfer to a different, cold, cold holding center. Other officers, Border Patrol? Hard to keep track of. Then, her mother had told her, a bus that dropped them in Mexico, an agent that said, "Make your way to El Salvador from here." They never did.

She heard the shore before she saw it. Heard the footsteps of others who reached the bank and abandoned their tires. So much mingled sorrow, relief. How nice it would be to . . . collapse. Rest awhile. She couldn't. She stood on the pebbly shore, the cold air shocking her skin into goose bumps, and kicked the tire aside with her leg. A rock had scratched her foot and she bled, but she had no time to worry over a small injury, minor pain. She blinked until she could make out a bush ahead and sprinted toward it, holding the bag and her throbbing arm at her side.

Behind the bush, Ana tore the plastic garbage bag and thrust her clothes on. She lamented she hadn't thought to bring a small towel. Her soaked bra formed rings on her T-shirt. Wet clothes a dead giveaway. She tried to dry herself as best she could with her one other, much dirtier, shirt. Ana put a sock over her cut foot and it quickly reddened with blood, slid into her crusty sneakers. Then, she made her way toward a sandy path, some houses farther ahead, highway, a dollar store, fast food. She moved through the scrub.

An engine whir and the screech of tires. She remained hidden but could see through the leaves. A few meters from her, a white van turned on its lights near another trail. Two men with flashlights and bulletproof vests jumped out from either side. They aimed the flashlights at three of the children.

She could hear their words, in Spanish. Questions about where they were coming from, whom else they were with.

The children in the light's halo were eight or nine, two boys and one girl. The girl's hair was sopping wet and she held a small black backpack with a broken strap. The kids looked at one another and slowly walked toward the agents, the girl dropping her backpack as if unsure what to do with it.

Ana became acutely aware of her breath, like she had no idea how she'd ever breathed without thinking about it, without measuring each inhale and exhale. Her whole body a spark. She wanted to run but had the better sense to stay hidden. She watched the agents' flashlights zoom above her as they made circles. She huddled deeper into the shadow of the bushes before her and thought of the promise she'd made her mother before she died—she'd survive, she'd fight. She told herself to swallow. She told herself to breathe.

They rounded up the rest of the children. Ana knew the parents instructed their kids to purposely look for the agents, to go to them. All sorts of rumors—they wouldn't send children back, they'd process asylum more quickly for a child without a parent or a parent with a child, they'd send them straight to their families if they had someone in the country. None of it was true or all of it was true.

So much silence and the mind became unbearable. She'd cried quietly many nights on the floor of drop houses and motels all over Tamaulipas, San Luis Potosí, Monterrey. Cancer had ripped through her mother so fast, there was little time to consider something so frivolous as *loss*. What a luxurious thing, to *feel*. The pain a tender ache now that she could massage and curl into. For so long, she'd held the grief at bay. She'd smiled strong for her mother as she walked her brittle body down the corridor of a clinic or placed the ventilator over her mouth. She'd pretended that, when her mother coughed and the tissue came away wet and blood spattered, there was still possibility, a chance for recovery. Her very job, Ana thought, had been *not* to grieve, so that her mother could. She'd been the airy balance in a world of plastic tubes, breathing machines, metal. On her silent trip, Ana had allowed the weeping child through, a child as alone in the world without her mother as she had been six years ago.

She remembered: her neighbor who took her in for a few days. A brief moment, a small act, but ingrained in the way childhood becomes a series of images, a detail, a color, a word so that one moment becomes a defining moment and you're not even sure why. *J*-something, absentmindedly slicking gloss over her lips, scrunching her hair with fruity mousse each morning. *J*-something's house, an exact replica of her mother's but bare, devoid of any decoration or personality. She remembered how, before she knew anything of what was to come, she'd curled in bed with her and they'd laughed together.

She'd felt so guilty and anxious, even as a child confused about what happened, the thought that police had taken her without a word to this woman, that this woman had probably wondered for the rest of her life what had happened to Ana. The police always did things like that. Enemy. *J*-something must have been in her room when the officers came. She never came out. Ana thought of trying to find her online, years later, to explain. But Ana had spent only a handful of days with this woman; it seemed silly, an imposition even. And yet, when Ana first thought of returning to the United States, where she had no family, this stranger had inexplicably popped into her mind. Maybe she just wanted to thank her. For softening the blow.

Ana doubted she'd ever see her again, but she was going to make her way to her old neighborhood anyway. At least she'd be in Miami, where the terrain was the tiniest bit more familiar. Where she'd sourced those childhood flashes.

Where high schools were used to girls with no parents and no social security numbers.

Ana could hear some of the children crying as the agents loaded them onto the van. She could hear one of the women saying, this is my daughter. One of the men saying, no, there's no one else. She could hear muffled sounds from the agents' walkie-talkies and the slamming of van doors. By the time the van's engine roared and the lights disappeared, she wanted nothing more than to fold into the dirt and sleep. But she couldn't stop now. How long before there were other vans? Men searching for tracks?

Right now there were no other vans, no other men, just the houses, the stores. An abandoned fishing pole, an abandoned Styrofoam cooler. Almost perverse, these marks of leisurely afternoons, maybe a splash in the river, the flick of a wrist. She wondered how many families looked across the river and thought of girls like her, said to themselves, *Thank God that's not us.* If life had taken only the slightest turn, she'd have thought that too.

The path snaked through the dark brush like a river cutting earth. She tried to remember the pollero's instructions, right—no, left—a highway? Lights ahead cast shadows over the ground like prison bars, and Ana could feel a false safety beckoning: *Crawl into the light.* How long since she'd slept a full night? How long since she'd—?

The adrenaline rush faded, only exhaustion in its wake, she couldn't even finish a thought. Up ahead she heard the rush of a single car.

———·———

The Amtrak train dropped her in Hialeah after three days and who knew how many transfers. Of all the train terminals she had passed through, this one struck her as saddest of all. A convergence point for south and west, tired bodies, people who couldn't afford plane tickets or had accrued too many DUIs to drive down. A man with a long red beard hoisted a duffel emblazoned with a Confederate flag onto his shoulder. A woman dragged three crying children who clung to her legs.

Ana emerged blinking into the violent sunlight. A fading, sun-bleached mural on one wall of the train station depicted the Miami she'd harbored in dreams, all swaying palm trees and impossibly blue sky, sky that bled into ocean until you couldn't tell where one ended and the other began. A metal cage covered half the mural and protected the air conditioner inside from theft. Beyond the train station, Ana could make out factory plumes and warehouses intersected by highway and the Miami-Dade Metrorail.

She'd done her research and knew she could take the Metrorail to Kendall and from there a bus to her old complex. She had the money all counted out in another ziplock in her backpack. She walked to the Hialeah station, passing boarded-up business fronts, check-cashing stores, pawnshops. Comforting, the Salvadoran pupusa spot, tucked between two abandoned buildings beneath an overpass. She couldn't see inside, because someone had painted a countryside landscape complete with a horse carriage over the glass. Flyers for various performers and club nights were tacked over rolling hills. But she could smell the masa, the refried beans, childhood.

On the Metrorail, she sat between high schoolers making their way home from school, boisterous and happy and ignoring her, and downtown workers in suits reading books or staring blankly. Ana had taken improvised sink baths in terminal bathrooms, but she knew she looked a little wild. Sticky, salty. Her stomach rumbled.

Miami roared into a blur below—used-car lots, sprawling malls, pastel-colored condo complexes with pools and tennis courts, squat houses with metal bars, front yards strewn with broken appliances, corroding playgrounds. In the horizon, so many cranes rose into the sky like beanstalks, half-finished high-rises in their jaws. When night descended, the whole city lit up in purple and blue and white, an explosion of color.

Her stop was a mall parking lot, in the shadow of department stores and luxury jewelers. The bus snaked down Kendall Drive in the dark, and she recognized little. Every strip mall was different, full of businesses she didn't remember. There were no more open spaces, big green lots. Every space filled by a new rental complex or a new strip mall or a new chain restaurant.

What would she even say? If she knocked on the door and the neighbor answered? If a stranger did?

She'd thought she'd be able to remember the path to her old home but was glad she carried an address with her. Nothing struck her as familiar—the whole complex was smaller than she remembered, grubbier than she remembered. She had expected a feeling—of home, a place in the world?—but it didn't come. All she felt was *tired*.

She made her way to what would have been her neighbor's door, walking past streetlights and feral cats, people walking dogs. It was April, but one patio was still strewn with Christmas lights. Little barbecues. Bougainvillea, birds-of-paradise. Many windows had the X-marks of masking tape. She remembered her mother doing this to prevent flying glass if a hurricane blew the windows. She knew hurricanes wouldn't arrive for months.

An older woman answered the door. She had bleached-blond hair pulled back into a severe bun. A hollowed look, dark rings under her eyes.

"I'm so sorry to bother," Ana said, hearing the accent she'd acquired after so many years in Mexico. "I'm looking for someone who used to live here. Years ago. It's possible she doesn't live here anymore?"

The woman towered over her. She looked down and then beyond Ana, as if distracted. "Are you looking for Jeanette?" she said in a small voice that didn't fit her.

Ana was taken aback. She'd already settled for disappointment. She'd already wondered what bus bench she'd sleep on, where she'd find a job when she didn't find this *J*-person. It'd been an impractical plan, she could admit it to herself.

"Yes," she said, hearing the anticipation and hope in her own voice. "Does she still live here?"

The woman didn't meet her eyes. She brought a hand to her collar. Beyond her, Ana could see the town house was near empty, just a few pieces of furniture. "Who did you say you were?"

It was a simple enough question, but Ana fumbled to answer. She said something about a night at her neighbor's house and a missing mother. She said something about years in Mexico and a grandmother in El Salvador.

The woman's eyes darted back to her. "I know you!" she gasped. The woman fumbled excitedly, or tensely, Ana couldn't tell. She didn't wait for Ana to say anything else, just led her into the house and began to brush crumbs off a kitchen table and rifle through cabinets to set a plate of food with a nervous energy that put Ana on edge.

But Ana was relieved to sit in the air-conditioning, to eat Cuban croquetas. She hadn't seen those in years.

The woman sat across from her, stared. Ana couldn't remember what this house had looked like so many years ago, but she was sure the table was the same. The woman picked at her nails and stared out the window at the empty unkempt lawn, at the cars parked in their designated lots.

"You said you knew me?" Ana was so hungry and couldn't take a bite.

The woman asked Ana why she was there, grew wide-eyed when Ana told her the story of where she'd been just days before. Ana hesitated when she said she wasn't sure where she would spend the night, but the woman interrupted right away.

"You can spend the night here," she said. "You can stay as long as you need to."

Ana thanked her profusely, this woman she did not even know, but she was suspicious at the way she darted questions, at times couldn't sit still and at others would quiet suddenly, seemed to disappear into her own mind, couldn't even tell her how she knew her.

As the woman took the empty plate before Ana to the sink and rinsed the crumbs, she finally introduced herself as Carmen. "I am Jeanette's mother," she said, back to Ana. "I'm sorry to tell you this, Ana, but Jeanette died." Carmen shut off the faucet and turned to face her. A cat Ana hadn't noticed hopped off the windowsill and extended into a stretch.

Ana swallowed. "Died?" The cat darted off.

Carmen had tears in her eyes. Her bottom lip trembled.

Ana looked down at the table. She hadn't known Jeanette, not at all, but for so many months, she'd harbored this silly fantasy of a distant friend in her childhood world. She searched for words. "I'm so—"

"Overdose," Carmen said, and shut off the water. She gripped the edge of the counter and bent her head.

Ana tried to conjure an image of Jeanette, tried to form a story about her life in all the years she hadn't seen her.

She realized addiction wouldn't have figured into her story. "I'm—" She wanted so badly to sleep, to will away the last few months, to have her mother again. "I'm so sorry," she said, angry at her own mechanical language.

"There is something else," Carmen said. Her mascara ran now, splotches down her cheeks. "It was me," Carmen said, "who encouraged her to call the police on you. I think it is my fault you were deported."

Ana lifted her head. Beyond the kitchen, she could see the empty living room through the pass-through. Just a couch and a sliding glass door. The cat pawing at the door.

"What? The police? She told them to take me?"

"It was so long ago," Carmen said. "What did I know then of what was right? What did I know then of what the world is capable of?"

Ana didn't know whether she spoke about the death of her daughter, or Ana's story. The air-conditioning sputtered on. How quickly a story unravels, an image blurs.

"Do you live here now?" Ana said because she could think of nothing else to say.

For so long, she'd had a different story about her own trajectory. She marveled at the way memory became static history, this thing so easily manipulated and shaped by her own desires. She had wanted to believe that Jeanette was a soft landing before the shock of detention, of deportation, all those years before. She had wanted to believe Jeanette kind. What did *she* know of other people? Of what they do?

"I suppose you could say that," Carmen said, dabbing at her eyes with a napkin. "She rented this house because she couldn't live with me anymore. And now I can't seem to leave it. I bought it. I can't seem to go home to my own big, empty house. I have no one left."

"I have no—" Ana started to say, but then stopped herself.

The arrangement was supposed to be temporary. Ana was only thirteen, after all. Carmen deemed it irresponsible to let her live alone in the house indefinitely. Carmen had lived there only part of the time. But now she took all her things back to Coral Gables and made no mention of moving back. Months bleeding into months. Carmen helped Ana enroll at the local high school, the high school Jeanette herself had attended. But Ana wasn't looking for a savior and wasn't looking to save anyone else; she'd learned in Mexico how easily a person in a certain position over her could build that kind of story for themselves. She lied about her age and found a job as a dishwasher at a restaurant. School, work, five hours of sleep each night. Day after day. She offered money to Carmen for rent, but Carmen didn't take the cash.

Ana didn't actually see her that often, though Carmen did check in on her from time to time. Ana didn't know how to feel about her, this woman who never knew her life. Who'd endangered it. She chalked up Carmen's absence to memory, Ana embodying something Carmen wanted to forget perhaps.

But on Ana's fifteenth birthday, Carmen gifted her an antique book. A copy of *Les Misérables* in Spanish, a first edition. Carmen said that after her own mother died, a niece in Cuba sent the book through a courier for Jeanette. This was months before her daughter's death. Carmen hadn't wanted to give the book to Jeanette, because she knew that after her relapse, she might sell it. Carmen said her niece in Cuba had remembered Jeanette loved the book during her last visit to the island, had remembered how she flipped its worn pages.

In the margin of one page, Carmen showed her, was Jeanette's handwriting below another note in faded script that seemed to spell out the same thing. *We are force*, the scribble read. And then Jeanette had added her own words, *We are more than we think we are.*

And though Ana had no idea why Jeanette had written those words, she chose to believe the sentence, the scribble, was a cry across time. Women? Certain women? We are more than we think we are. There was always *more*. She had no idea what else life would ask of her, force out of her, but right then, there was cake and candles and this, a gift. She thought that she, too, might give away the book someday, though she had no idea to whom. Someone who reminded her of herself maybe. Someone drawn to stories. She said thank you and put the book aside.

ACKNOWLEDGMENTS

Thank you, Megan Lynch, for your unwavering support, for making this book better, for ushering it into the world during the strangest of times with so much grace and vision.

Thank you, PJ Mark and Marya Spence, for being a literal dream team and my style icons. Thank you for being so fierce and dedicated and thoughtful.

Thank you, Michael Taeckens, for your zeal and your kindness and your patience, for bringing so much beautiful energy into the publication of this book.

Thank you, Lauren Bittrich, Amelia Possanza, Katherine Turro, Nancy Trypuc, Nadxieli Nieto, and everyone at Flatiron and Macmillan. Thank you, Natalie Edwards, Ian Bonaparte, and the whole team at Janklow & Nesbit. Thank you, Katy Lasell and Broadside PR.

Thank you, Roxane Gay, for your unwavering belief in this book and my writing throughout so many years. Your mentorship and guidance have shaped me in ways both large and small. I am forever changed.

Thank you, Sharon Solwitz, for your keen eye and unwavering honesty, for always believing the best version of this book was within my grasp.

Thank you, Brian Leung, for sparking my unlikely foray into elements of historical fiction and for seeing my potential. Thank you to the Purdue M.F.A. program and to Marianne Boruch, Don Platt, Kaveh Akbar, and Terese Marie Mailhot. Thank you, Adrian Matejka and Dana Roeser, for being the first to call me a poet. Thank you, Al Lopez, for taking me under your wing. Thank you, Jeff Amos, Laura Lee, Robert Powers, Samantha Atkins, Hannah Rahimi, Juliana Goodman, Diana Clarke, John Milas, Carey Compton, Megan Denton Ray, Mitchell Jacobs, Alex Stinton, Noah Baldino, Charles Peck, Caleb Milne, and Hannah Dellabella.

Thank you to the Rona Jaffe Foundation, the Martha Heasley Cox Center for Steinbeck Studies at San Jose State University, the Indiana Arts Commission, Bread Loaf Writers' Conference, Community of Writers at Squaw Valley, Lighthouse Works, and Sarabande Books for your critical support that made writing this book possible.

Thank you to all of the organizers I ever crossed paths with in the years that shaped some of this writing, in particular my compañerxs at UltraViolet and Presente. Thank you to the latter for continuing the work with Dignidad Literaria. To all of the families I met in deportation defense work, to all of the women of Karnes, thank you for your fight.

Thank you to Casa Víctor Hugo in La Habana, Association Cuba Cooperation France, and the University of Miami Cuban Heritage Collection archives.

Thank you to everyone who read early portions of this novel and provided invaluable feedback, especially Diego Iñiguez-Lopez, Yareli Urbina, Christine Vines, Robert Powers, Jake Zucker, Jesus Iñiguez, Iraida H. Lopez, Alexander Chee, Carmen Maria Machado, and Oscar Villalon.

Mi gente de Cuba: este libro no hubiera sido posible sin ustedes. Tío Jorge, gracias por creer siempre en mí y por el gran regalo de un segundo hogar lleno de tanto amor, cariño, y jodienda. Te adoro. Gracias tío Pablito y Ramses. Gracias a Sara, Lina, Madelín, Ariel, Neisy, Robney y todas mis amistades cubanas. Yolanda, Yolita, Rosa y Yoan, siempre los llevo en mi corazón.

Gracias a toda mi familia de Méxíco, en especial mi abuela Raquel, mi hermana Geraldine, y mis sobrinos Toñito, Valentina, y Fer. Gracias a Brenda, Conchis, Carlos, Pope, Andrea, Carlitos, Popito, Alejandra y todo el resto de mi familia. Tía Susie, abuelo Porfirio, y Chuchito, los extraño cada día.

Thank you, Yaneris and Zoila. Thank you, Domingo, Aasheekaa, Lala, Megan, Frank, and Kelvin. Thank you, Jake, for being a steady source of support through every single stage of this journey.

Thank you, Amanda, Tía, Allie, Diego, Ofe, Toty, and Lilia. Thank you, Dad, An, and Maya. Thank you, Frida. Gracias Abuelita por todo. THANK YOU, Mami, for everything.

PLEASE NOTE: In order to provide reading groups with the most informed and thought-provoking questions possible, it is necessary to reveal important aspects of the plot of this novel—as well as the ending. If you have not finished reading *Of Women and Salt* by Gabriela Garcia, we respectfully suggest that you may want to wait before reviewing this guide.

Of Women and Salt
DISCUSSION QUESTIONS

1. The novel begins with this sentence: "Jeanette, tell me that you want to live." How does this intimate direct address from mother to daughter set the tone for some of the themes we encounter in the following pages?

2. María Isabel loses two of the most important people in her life and gives birth to her daughter, Cecilia. In what way does the concept of loss continue to impact/inform the decisions these women make?

3. The story exposes the flaws and inequities in the immigration system. How did Gloria's deportation become a catalyst for this story?

4. Compare and contrast the mother-daughter relationships in this novel. What are some of the differences? And what are the similarities?

5. The first-edition copy of *Les Misérables* appears in multiple scenes; the first time we see the book is in Cuba in 1866, and the last time we see it is in present-day Miami. What do you think the author is trying to say about the way stories transcend generations?

6. Which chapter surprised you the most, and why?

7. How did you feel about jumping through time and place in this novel? Discuss the importance of narratives that defy chronological/sequential order.

8. What is the significance of the recurring phrase "We are force"?

9. Think about the sections where the character is speaking from their first-person point of view. Why do you think the author allows certain characters—like Gloria and Maydelis—to tell us their stories in their own voices instead of narrating from a distant third-person narrator?

10. What did you think of the novel's ending? Could things have turned out differently for Jeanette? How?